DEADLY CARGO

"How'd your friend die?" asked the red-haired man.

"Smallpox," McCutcheon said. "Worst case I ever seen. Sure hope I ain't caught it myself, though I fear I have."

"Are you sure that your friend there died of smallpox? Because I'm kind of worried now that maybe I might catch it. So I'd like to see for myself, just to know for sure what the facts is."

"The coffin's nailed shut."

"How long's he been dead?"

"Three days," Sampson spoke up, to McCutcheon's displeasure.

"Three days?" The red-haired man looked deeply skeptical. "Mighty odd we don't smell him then." He leveled his shotgun, aiming it at McCutcheon's middle. "I want to see your dead friend. It may be there's not a dead man at all in there. There's other things that can be carried in a wood box."

The coffin top burst upward so suddenly that even McCutcheon and Sampson were startled.

The man with the shotgun turned his weapon toward Jake Penn, who sat upright like a reanimated corpse, boths hands wrapped around pistol butts. . . .

Ransom Riders

JUDSON GRAY

A SIGNET BOOK

SIGNET
Published by New American Library, a division of
Penguin Putnam Inc., 375 Hudson Street,
New York, New York 10014, U.S.A.
Penguin Books Ltd, 80 Strand,
London WC2R ORL, England
Penguin Books Australia Ltd, Ringwood,
Victoria, Australia
Penguin Books Canada Ltd, 10 Alcorn Avenue,
Toronto, Ontario, Canada M4V 3B2
Penguin Books (N.Z.) Ltd, 182–190 Wairau Road,
Auckland 10, New Zealand

Penguin Books Ltd, Registered Offices:
Harmondsworth, Middlesex, England

First published by Signet, an imprint of New American Library,
a division of Penguin Putnam Inc.

First Printing, November 2001
10   9   8   7   6   5   4   3   2   1

To Frank Wheeler

Part I

The Mission

Chapter One

Jim McCutcheon topped the hillock a little faster than Jake Penn, and thus was the first to come in view of the big house in the flat valley below.

He pulled his black horse to a halt and let out a slow whistle as Penn, astride his big roan, rode up and stopped beside him.

"Penn, that surely is the house of a very rich man," McCutcheon said.

"I told you you'd be impressed," Penn said. He leaned over, spit out an amber dollop of tobacco juice, and resettled the raw-tasting plug against his jaw. "You'll not find a finer home in all of Texas than that of Abel Blain."

"I still can't understand why a man so well off would be a friend to a penniless drifter like you."

"Abel and me, we got history together. War history. That draws men close to one another."

"Close enough that you're confident he'll give us work?"

"If he's got work, he'll provide it. And there's always something needing doing at so big a ranch."

"I hope so. Because we're going to be down to eating our boots before long if we don't make some money." McCutcheon examined the big house and the grounds around it a few moments more. "How'd he get so much money, anyway?" he asked.

"Great success in the cattle business, added on top

of an inheritance from his wife's uncle, who had developed railroads in the East. When the uncle died, Abel went from being a common Kentucky horse farmer to a rich man in the breadth of a single day."

"I wish I could have a day like that. Just one. That's all I'd ask."

"Well, Abel puts on no airs, but I know the opportunities the money gave them made them very happy. He and Sarah moved to Texas after the money came to them, and had good years here. Of course, with Sarah having died so young, it took the best part of his happiness away. I've heard him say he'd give up all he has if he could just get her back."

"But he's not fully alone, right? You said that the little girl is still with him."

"Yes. Bethany Colby, Sarah's little cousin. They never had children of their own, but they raised Bethany like she was their own daughter." Penn chuckled. " 'Little cousin,' I called her. It ain't true any more. Bethany's no little girl now. She'd already grown into a beautiful young woman last time I saw her. Now, I suppose, she's a true lady."

"Well! I look forward to meeting her."

"You behave yourself, Cutch. I'll whop you like a balking mule if you so much as give her an improper glance."

"I'll be downright saintly, I promise. But tell me this: Was Bethany the daughter of the railroad man who died and made them rich?"

"Oh, no. She was the daughter of the railroad man's brother, as a matter of fact. A poor man, Abel told me, and given to drink, which probably killed him. But he'd have probably died young, anyway. Dying young runs in the Colby family, according to Abel. Heart trouble. That's what killed Sarah."

The panorama before them was lighted by the late afternoon sun. Beyond the big, multigabled house—

which was very nearly a mansion, especially by the standards of 1870s frontier Texas—stood a big bunkhouse, no less than three barns, a few stables, a tack shed, two smokehouses, a large chicken house, and various other outbuildings. A sprawling corral was surrounded by a fence painted brilliant white, spread out between the house and the creek, which ran off into the distance toward the Rio Grande.

McCutcheon said, "That's a big place for one man and one young lady to fill up all by theirselves."

"Abel's got his housekeepers. And his ranch hands all around, of course. It's generally a busy place around here."

"I don't see much going on at the moment."

"Roundup time. The ranch is mostly empty, cowboys out on the range."

"Well, dang it, we've come too late for work, then."

"Oh, there'll be other work. Or Abel might send us out to catch up with the herd."

McCutcheon squinted from underneath the brim of a wide, battered hat. He still looked like the young man he once was, though his skin was beginning to weather after months on the move with Jake Penn. He'd lived the drifter's life even before taking up with Penn, and McCutcheon could barely recall the last time he'd slept indoors. Still, he had no regrets. His life had been better since he'd taken up with Jake Penn. He didn't mind the stares and comments he sometimes received from those who wondered why a young white man would keep company with a middle-aged black man such as Jake. McCutcheon had learned a valuable lesson from Penn: It doesn't so much matter what others think of a man, as what that man thinks of himself.

Penn said, "Let's go down and say howdy to Abel."

They rode down the hillock and toward the sprawling ranch. It was dry, as there had been no rain for a long time, and their horses kicked up plumes of dust with each step.

They had just ridden past the board fence that marked off the beginning of the substantially grassless yard when a tall, strongly built man with a weathered, aging face, wearing the clothing of a cattleman strode out of the house and eyed them closely. His expression initially was wary, but he brightened with surprise to see Penn. McCutcheon assumed this man was Abel Blain, though he was older than he'd expected Blain to be.

"Jake Penn?" the man exclaimed. "Is that you? Lord have mercy, man! Good to see you!"

The man advanced, slowly, limping noticeably, already putting out his hand even as Penn dismounted.

Penn shook the man's hand. The fingers felt oddly gnarled. The other man barely restrained a full wince at Penn's squeezing of his hand.

"Hello, Will Lincoln," Penn said. "I didn't expect to see you. Figured you'd be out on roundup."

The man shook his head. "I'm just too old and wore out for it, Jake. The old joints are beginning to twist up on me and hurt, as you can see. I'm limited to doing most of my work here on the grounds now. Abel ought to pasture me out like the old horse I am, but he's a kindhearted man, as you know. He keeps me around, keeps me working at what I can."

"You're not foreman now?"

"No. Abel's got a man named Keith Dresden doing that for him these days."

"I'm sorry to see you slowing down, Will. Is everything well with you besides the rheumatiz?"

The man gazed at Penn a couple of beats, then shook his head slowly. "No. I'd be lying if I said it was."

"What's wrong?"

Lincoln cast a suspicious glance at McCutcheon.

"It's all right," Penn said. "He's my partner. You can talk in front of him, whatever it is."

Still Lincoln hesitated. "In this situation, it's not really my place to speak to anyone. Not even you, Jake. It's Abel's place to do that, if he chooses." He paused, then forced up a grin again. "It truly is good to see you again, Jake. But that you should show up at a time like this . . . Lord have mercy! Who'd have expected it?" He shook his head. "Let me get the little Mex boy around to see to your horses."

Will Lincoln limped around the house, doing his best despite his arthritis, shouting for somebody named Pablo.

Chapter Two

McCutcheon dismounted. "And just who is Will Lincoln?"

"An old friend. Ranch foreman here for years. He's getting mighty crippled up, ain't he? I hate to see it."

"Something is wrong here, Jake, as I'm sure you could tell from the way he talked."

"Yeah."

"That man has a great weight of worry on him."

Penn glanced at McCutcheon. "You know, Jim, I believe you're starting to mature up a little. You're getting to be what they call perceptive."

Preceded by a small-framed Mexican boy, Will Lincoln came back around the house. "This is Pablo," he said. "He'll see to your horses."

Penn and McCutcheon nodded greetings to the boy, who was too shy to look them in the eyes.

"Is Abel inside?" Penn asked.

"Yes."

"Reckon he's in the humor to take visitors?"

"I believe he'd be glad to see *you*, Jake." He glanced at McCutcheon, then back at Penn.

McCutcheon noticed, and felt a faint twinge of insult. Was Lincoln implying that only Penn was welcome here?

Penn said, "We figured to ask if there might be some work around the place that Jim and me here could do for him. We're a bit down on our luck just now, to be honest, Will."

Will Lincoln was very somber. "If it's luck you're after, you've come to the wrong place."

"There's no jobs to be done?"

For some reason, Lincoln laughed at that. "Oh, there's a job to be done. Quite a job indeed! But there's already seven men set to do it . . . and you should count yourself lucky you ain't one of them."

The man's talking riddles, McCutcheon thought. He glanced at Penn, who seemed equally perplexed.

"Will, just what's going on here?" Penn asked.

"I'm not at liberty to tell you of my own volition. But maybe Abel will—if you really want the burden of knowing. Just hold tight a minute while I go tell him Jake Penn's come to see him."

Lincoln walked back into the house, leaving Penn and McCutcheon to try to figure out what could possibly account for all this odd behavior and cryptic talk. McCutcheon began to wish they hadn't come.

Less than a minute later, Lincoln reemerged.

"Come on in, Penn. Abel's surprised you're here, but mighty glad you are."

Penn and McCutcheon headed toward the door. But Lincoln put out his hand toward McCutcheon. "Just Penn . . . sorry, young man. Abel doesn't want to see nobody he doesn't know just now. No offense."

McCutcheon, though, did take offense. "What's wrong? Is Jake's word about my character not good enough for you?"

Penn turned to his partner. "Cutch, just give it a minute and keep your shirt on. Have yourself a smoke. I'll find out what's going on. There may be a good reason for this."

"I hope so. Because I know when I've been slighted."

Penn sighed. Still too hotheaded, his young partner was. Maybe patience could only be learned with age.

"Just stay put, Jim. I'll be back out in a minute."

McCutcheon nodded and grunted a reluctant agreement, then watched sullenly as Penn and Will Lincoln walked through the door. Lincoln closed it behind them.

McCutcheon turned away, walking across the porch and into the yard as he dug into a pocket for his tobacco pouch and rolling papers.

The ornate front parlor of the Blain house was bigger than all of the dwellings Penn had occupied throughout his entire life. He worked his way slowly around the room, refamiliarizing himself with furnishings and decorations he'd not seen for a few years, and noting some he thought were new.

It was easier to look at his surroundings than at the shocking sight of Abel Blain.

Blain, thin and weak and hardly the man Penn had known for years, was at the moment sipping something medicinal from a cup with the help of Will Lincoln. Penn had seen men laid out for burial who looked healthier than Blain looked just now.

Obviously Will Lincoln wasn't the only man here who had declined dramatically since Penn had been here last.

But the house was as much a spectacle as ever. Beneath Penn's feet were Oriental rugs, and all around him sat mahogany furniture. A shining white-glazed grand piano stood in the middle of the room.

Penn studied the large oil paintings around the walls. No mere copies were these paintings. Fine originals, all of them, hung on walls covered with expensive paper above wainscotting of stained walnut.

Above the mantle was the most eye-catching painting of them all: a portrait of a dark-haired, dark-eyed young woman of sublime beauty. The artist had caught a devilish flash in the eyes of Abel's niece, Bethany Colby, that made Penn smile. He'd seen the real-life version of that flash many times, even when Bethany was a little girl.

Blain finished his medicine and leaned back in his chair. Penn turned, approached him, and knelt, bringing himself down to the level of the seated Blain.

"Abel, what's happened to you?" he asked forthrightly.

"Almost too much to tell, Jake."

"You're ill."

"Yes. And crippled, too. Ironic, isn't it? Will getting like he is, and me even worse. But in my case it was a riding accident. I'll not walk again without a crutch or a cane, or so the doctors tell me. But they worry more about the illness than the injury."

"What's wrong with you?"

Blain waved his hand and shook his head. "It doesn't matter. It's nothing anyone else can catch. And I'm actually getting better now, slowly, even though I was very sick for a long time." His voice, once rich and deep, was now frail and soft. This man was a human rag with most of the vitality wrung out of him.

"Abel, from some things Will said, I have the impression that something is wrong here. And not just illness and so on. Am I right?"

Abel frowned silently at Penn, then answered with a question of his own. "What inspired you to visit just now, Jake?"

"I wanted to see you and Bethany and everybody again." With Blain so pitiful, Penn found he couldn't admit up front that the dominating reason he'd come was a desperate need for work.

Abel closed his eyes. "Bethany," he said. "Bethany."

That gave Penn a chill. "Abel, is something wrong with Bethany?"

Abel opened his eyes. "Are you in need of work just now, Jake?"

The question surprised him. Maybe Blain had seen through him. "Well . . . yes."

"I ask you that because it so happens there's a job that has to be done. An ugly and maybe a dangerous one. Are you interested?"

"Well . . . I'd like to hear more."

"Very well. I only hope you don't regret it afterward. Because once you hear what I tell you, and understand what must be done, I'll ask you to make a decision. If you say yes to what I ask of you, there are some other men elsewhere in this house tonight whom you'll meet."

"This job sounds mighty important."

"A more important job you could never imagine," Blain replied. "I only wish I was able to do it myself."

McCutcheon strolled the ranch grounds, smoking and wondering what was happening inside the house.

He circled the house, and caught a glimpse of the interior of the front room through a side window where a curtain was only partially closed. He saw a painting of a beautiful woman hanging on the wall.

McCutcheon stared at it until the cigarette hanging on his lip burned down until it nearly scorched him, making him spit it onto the ground.

What a portrait! He'd never seen such a beautiful image. Not knowing who was portrayed, he wondered if this might be Blain's late wife, Sarah.

Maybe it was that niece of hers, Bethany Colby. If the latter, the real-life version was probably somewhere in that house right now. Which only made McCutcheon all the more resentful at being left outside.

He moved a few steps to one side and through the same window saw Penn sitting in a chair, leaning forward, apparently listening to someone. Abel Blain, probably. But McCutcheon couldn't find an angle to allow him to see the person to whom Penn spoke.

He left the window and went on around the rear of the house. There he saw a stocky woman walking toward the chicken house, hatchet in hand. Over at the tack shed, a skinny Mexican man was donning a leather apron, ready to go to work on a saddle. McCutcheon nodded at both of them, trying to be friendly, but they stared back at him as if afraid. The woman hurried away so fast one would have thought a quick rain shower had set in.

McCutcheon walked back around to the front of the house, wondering if he looked dangerous. He was being roundly rejected everywhere he turned.

It was enough to hurt a man's feelings.

He sat down on the edge of the front porch, smoking and waiting for Penn.

Chapter Three

The sun was setting when Penn finally emerged from the house.

Determined not to show just how curious he was, McCutcheon didn't acknowledge Penn's appearing, and just stared at the northern horizon.

"Cutch, you and me need to talk," Penn said. His tone was solemn.

"Do we?" McCutcheon replied.

"I've been hired to a job here."

"Really? And let me guess the rest: I ain't."

"It wasn't my decision for it to be that way, Cutch."

"I'm sure. Well, what's your job?"

"Can't tell you."

"Huh?"

"Abel's made me promise to say nothing. And there's good reason for it."

McCutcheon glared at Penn, and lost the battle to not show his perturbance. "Do I look like some sort of horse thief or something? I'm feeling downright unwelcome here! I'm not allowed in the house, not told nothing about what's going on . . . even the hired help here gives me the evil eye! Now my own partner is refusing even to tell me what job he's been hired to!"

"I can't help that. I told you: It ain't my choice to make."

McCutcheon forced himself to cool off. He drew in

a deep breath. "Ah, well. I'll just not worry about it, then. I'll just go off and look for a few dead bugs to eat so I can stretch my starvation out as long as possible. Never you mind about me."

"I'm sorry. I really am."

McCutcheon stood, paced around a bit, then stopped. "Jake, I thought we were partners. You're actually willing to cut me out?"

"Abel would hire only me."

"What kind of job is this?"

"A . . . private one."

"Right. And you can't say more because Abel Blain made you promise."

"That's right."

"You sure let this Blain fellow dictate a lot of terms to you, you know it? What's wrong with you, Penn? Did you decide to go back to being a slave again and make Abel Blain your master?"

Penn's stare instantly turned colder than winter steel, and when he spoke his voice was different than before. "Don't ever say anything like that to me again, Jim. Never again. There's some kinds of talk I refuse to hear. Even from you."

McCutcheon let his gaze sink to the ground. "I'm sorry, Jake. That was uncalled for."

Penn grunted.

McCutcheon looked up and added, "But you could have told him you'd not do the job without me."

"Not in this case. If you knew, you'd understand. I really wish I could tell you."

"What's Blain got against me?"

"Nothing. This is just a job he wants done by those he knows well. He has to be extremely careful just now."

"How long will it take?"

"A few days, if all goes well. And it will pay me well. Pay *us* well, for you know I'm a sharing man."

Penn grinned, clearly trying to lighten the atmosphere. "Just like my mama taught me to be."

"What am I supposed to do in the meantime? You remember, I hope, that we have not even enough money to buy one man's food for more than a day or two."

Penn reached into his pocket and pulled out a stack of bills. He handed the money wordlessly to McCutcheon.

McCutcheon took it, and his mouth fell open. "There's more than three hundred dollars here, Jake."

"Abel gave it to me just now to give to you. I told him our situation. I said pretty much the same things you just said to me. So he gave me five hundred dollars. Two I've got with me, the other three for you."

McCutcheon pocketed the cash, pulled it out again for another quick glance, just to make sure it was real, then repocketed it. He couldn't find words.

"He's a rich man," Penn said, smiling. "It's easy for him to do things like that."

"What are you fellows going to do?" McCutcheon asked. "Go off and murder somebody or something?" He chuckled, but there just might have been a serious undertone in there somewhere, and Penn noted it.

Penn shook his head. "You know better than that."

McCutcheon eyed him closely. "But you do have a solemn manner about you, Jake. There's something about this that has you worried."

"It's a serious job."

"Five hundred dollars or not, if this job is something that's going to cause us trouble later on . . ."

"It won't cause us more trouble. In fact, it will make us more money. Abel plans to hand me, and every other man I'll be riding with, a thousand dollars when we finish the job."

"A thousand dollars! This truly must be some hellacious kind of job!"

"Just one that has to be done."

"Dangerous?"

"Yes. But there will be others with me. I haven't met them yet, but Abel says they're good men. They could have done the job without me, really."

"Then why are you included?"

"Abel says me showing up when I did seems to him to be a sign or a good omen or something. Like I'm supposed to be part of this."

"Do you believe that?"

Penn shrugged.

"When this job is through, are you going to be able then to tell me what it was?"

"I think so."

McCutcheon burned with curiosity. He also knew it was futile to pursue the matter at this point. When Jake Penn decided to hold a secret, it was as if that secret was locked in a bank vault.

"Where should I go while you're doing the job, Jake?"

"There's a little town near here to the west a few miles, called Black Hill. It's a sorry little place, but Abel says there are good accommodations to be had in a hotel he owns. Go there and have a rest. Sleep in a real bed for a few days, and fill up on food. When I'm finished with this, I'll come find you there."

"Are you going to be here at this ranch throughout?"

"No. I've got to travel. Into Mexico, I think."

McCutcheon wished he could know more, but knew that Jake would never tell anything he'd vowed not to reveal.

"You take care of yourself, Jake. Whatever the devil you're up to."

"I'll do my best. Now we've got to part company, Cutch. You go on to Black Hill. I've got to go back in. There's some men Abel's waiting to introduce me to."

*   *   *

Jim McCutcheon felt quite uncomfortable as he rode alone through the dark night, following a barely visible road toward the town of Black Hill, Texas.

Though he tried to persuade himself that Penn knew what he was doing, the whole situation just didn't feel right.

Something was amiss, and Penn's manner had showed it.

McCutcheon was weary, and when he was weary, he was capable of entertaining thoughts that otherwise would not be considered. He began to wonder, idly and then resentfully, if maybe this set of circumstances was somehow just an excuse for Jake to do something he'd wanted to do ever since the pair of them had taken to riding together. Maybe Penn had tired of his friendship and was brushing him aside, for good.

By the time he'd traveled another two miles, McCutcheon had dismissed these doubts. Whatever the questions and emotions of the moment, Penn's friendship with him was nothing false. In the months they'd ridden as partners, he and Penn had become as close as kin.

Whatever had led Jake Penn to push him aside tonight must be something important. Something Penn had no choice about.

But why the secrecy? What did Blain want to hide? When men hid things, they generally did so because those things, once exposed, could damage them.

The town of Black Hill began to materialize in the darkness ahead, as specks of light glinting out on the plains.

McCutcheon wondered how the word "hill" had ever found its way into the name of a place so flat. Probably, as was so often the case, the town was named after some other town in some distant state that happened to hold a sentimental significance to whomever had founded this settlement.

McCutcheon's tired horse, perhaps sensing a stable ahead, picked up its speed a little as the lights drew closer.

McCutcheon hadn't expected much of the town of Black Hill, and much indeed it didn't provide, but it did prove a little more substantial than he'd anticipated.

McCutcheon noticed several saloons, a school, a church, various general businesses, boarding houses, and one surprisingly large hotel. The only hotel in town.

THE BLAIN HOUSE, read the sign over the door.

McCutcheon dismounted, hitched his horse to a rail, and went inside. The money in his pocket made him feel flush but also wary. Little towns like this near the border often attracted a rough and dangerous element. He would be sure to keep his money out of sight as much as possible.

He stabled his horse at the nearby livery, then checked in.

The hotel room was large, the bed soft and deep. McCutcheon, though, was too weary of his trail-dirty condition to yield at once to the temptation to throw himself into that bed. He paid a little Mexican boy who worked around the place to bring him water and soap, then washed at his basin and changed into fresh long underwear. He gave his trousers, shirt, and vest a quick hand-laundering with the leftover washwater, and hung them in a corner to dry.

Only then did he sink into the bed, plunging deep in its feathery bulk.

Paradise!

He slept, but not for long. An aching back awakened him. He sat up, the bed moving under him like a blob of soft mud. Wincing, he pushed himself out of bed and stretched his back.

He'd forgotten that a man who has been sleeping

mostly on the hard ground for months could not suddenly shift into an overly soft bed without his back paying a price for it. Annoyed, he paced around the room, stretching and twisting his spine until the pain was mostly gone.

He pulled the feather tick off the bed and threw it on the floor. A hard surface beneath the soft mattress would make all the difference.

McCutcheon heard noise on the street outside just as he was about to lie down. Walking over to the window, he looked out of his dark room and saw men, some afoot and three on horseback, talking among themselves, their voices rising and falling. He couldn't really hear what was said, but could tell that the subject, whatever it was, generated great interest and excitement.

Then he heard two words he could clearly make out. Abel Blain.

McCutcheon suddenly had a bad feeling.

For the rest of the night he still found it difficult to sleep.

Chapter Four

Abel Blain, who had talked until his already weak voice was now barely a whisper, leaned forward and looked Penn in the eye as he spoke.

"You understand the entire situation now, Jake. You understand the risks on all sides. I've already asked you if you would help me, and you've already agreed . . . but now I ask you again. This is a final chance for you to turn away from what could be a dangerous task. If you choose to walk away, I'll not hold it against you. But I will have to ask you to maintain absolute secrecy in any case. Bethany's welfare may depend upon it. So now, Jake, I ask you: Will you help me, and Bethany, and take part in this mission?"

Behind Penn stood a group of seven men. He'd been introduced to them one by one. All were solemn. Some had seemed reasonably welcoming to him. Others—one in particular—hadn't.

That man, the ranch foreman Keith Dresden, stepped forward before Penn could answer Blain. He was a tall man, rugged, something close to handsome. But his looks were marred by a very large, jagged scar that ran down the left side of his face, crooked as a mountain river on a map.

"Abel, if I may speak . . ."

"Surely, Keith."

Dresden, whom Blain had introduced as leader of

the group, looked darkly at Penn for a moment, then back at Blain.

"Abel, I don't favor bringing this darky into this situation. I'll speak plainly. You can't trust his kind, in my experience, not even the best of them. And though you may know him, none of the rest of us do. I don't want unknowns riding with me . . . especially of his kind."

Silence lingered a few moments, then Blain replied softly. "You don't know Jake Penn, Keith, but I do. And you can believe me when I tell you you'll not have a better man, a better fighter, a braver or more reliable companion riding with you than Jake Penn. I had occasion to cross paths with this man as a fellow soldier during the late war, and he saved my skin. Twice."

"Just as you saved mine later," Penn cut in.

"Yes, but never mind that. The point, Keith, is that Jake Penn *will* be a part of this enterprise . . . if he wishes. I'll not have your ignorance about him—or your attitudes about his race—cause me to leave him out."

Blain began now to address Penn. "I've never been a praying man as much as I should be, I admit, Jake," he said. "But after I received the letter, and realized what had happened and what had to be done, I prayed hard. For Bethany's safety, and for any needed help to come to me. I already had seven good men to call upon. When you rode in, I believed right away that my prayer had been answered. Even so, you needn't go along if you don't wish to . . . but I hope you will."

Penn said, "You can count on me, Abel. I've already told you that."

Dresden made a barely audible, disdainful grunting sound.

"It will be dangerous," Blain said. "Especially if word of what you're doing gets out. I've tried to ensure it would not, but in my experience, such things seldom stay a secret."

"It won't the first time I've been in danger. You know that better than anybody, Abel."

Blain smiled and nodded, his eyes moistening. "Thank you, Jake. I feel sure now that you will succeed. I was hopeful before . . . now I'm downright confident."

Keith Dresden glared at Penn in silence, then turned and walked back to where he had stood before. He muttered something to one of the other men.

Penn wished Blain hadn't made that last comment. He could tell that Dresden resented seeing Blain cast so much good favor on this newcomer, thereby diminishing that which was previously attached to him. And the fact that Dresden was a blatant racist did nothing to better the situation.

"When will we leave?" Penn asked.

"As quickly as the horses are ready," Blain replied. "Had you arrived here much later than you did, you would have missed the chance to go along at all."

In Black Hill, McCutcheon greeted the next morning with the same unsettled feeling that had plagued his sleep.

The morning was bright, and the sun streamed through the curtained window, giving the room a cheery, friendly atmosphere. Yet still, McCutcheon remained troubled.

He threw his mattress back on the bed, then washed his face, upper body, and then his hair. Toweling off, he dressed and descended to the street, where he followed his nose to a café.

The food was delicious, served on a good china plate on a clean tabletop beside a window with small red and clear panes in a checkerboard pattern. He drank four cups of coffee and ate three extra biscuits

with molasses. Satisfying as it was both physically and
mentally to eat such a good meal in so pleasant a
setting, he couldn't squelch his sense of worry about
Penn.

He wished he knew what was going on at the
Blain ranch.

McCutcheon stewed over the mystery as he finished
his coffee, then rose and paid for his meal. After that
he hit the streets for a morning walk and some con-
templation.

He tried to talk himself out of worrying about Penn,
but his concerns only increased.

The prospect of remaining stuck here in this little
town for God only knew how long, wondering all the
while what was going on with Penn, was very unap-
pealing. McCutcheon appreciated a good hotel room
and restaurant food as much as any man. But not
while he was worried about his partner.

McCutcheon glanced across the street and noticed
a group of men talking to one another. It instantly
reminded him of the group he'd seen the night before.

On impulse, he walked near the talking group and
pretended to examine a stack of gardening tools rest-
ing out in front of a nearby mercantile store. He
couldn't hear much of what was said, but the words
"Blain ranch" came through, along with a reference
to "that pretty gal of his."

McCutcheon stared at the shovel he was holding.
Whatever had happened at Blain's spread, news—or,
at least, rumor—was getting out.

"Something wrong with that shovel, young man?"

McCutcheon jumped, startled by the shopkeeper,
who had come out the door without him noticing.

"Oh, no, no. Nothing wrong."

"Quite a frown you were giving it. I thought you'd
detected a flaw. If you want a shovel, young man,

I'll make sure it's in good condition before you take it away."

"No, I don't need a shovel just now. Just looking." He put the shovel back in place and started to turn away, but he paused. "Mister, can I ask you a question?"

"Fire away."

"I heard some folks talking about the Blain ranch . . . is something wrong there?"

"I don't know, quite honestly. I've heard some whispers, too, but I don't pay much heed to such." He puffed up a bit, self-righteously. "If it ain't my business, it ain't my business, and I close my ears to it."

A virtuous shopkeeper, obviously. Too bad, McCutcheon thought. A big-eared gossip would be more helpful at the moment.

"Thank you sir," McCutcheon said. "If I do decide to buy a shovel, this will surely be the place I'll come." He touched the brim of his hat and walked away.

McCutcheon strode across the street and continued his stroll around the little town. Passing a couple of old men whittling on a bench in front of a café, he heard the name "Blain" mentioned again. Going farther, he passed the just-opened doors of a gaming hall, and glanced inside. A couple of men who'd entered were huddled together, talking seriously. He could guess their subject. Slipping closer, he heard mention of a ranch, and "that poor girl."

His worries about Penn redoubled. Whatever had gone on at Blain's spread, it seemed that everyone knew much more about it than he did. Clearly it was fascinating enough to be the center of public gossip. Which probably meant it was significant . . . maybe dangerous, too.

And Penn was right in the midst of it.

A gun shop across the street had opened its doors a half hour earlier. McCutcheon sat down on a keg under a battered canvas awning jutting out over the boardwalk, and watched three hard-eyed men approach and enter the gun shop. Ten minutes later they emerged, each bearing brand-new rifles. One of them had a long scope mounted on his, much like a sharpshooter might carry.

They went to a hitchpost down the street, mounted the three blaze-faced horses tied there, and rode away in the general direction of the Blain spread, McCutcheon noted.

"Watch yourself, Jim McCutcheon," he whispered to himself. "Don't start jumping to conclusions you can't justify."

Three men had just purchased rifles, but what of it? There could be a hundred reasons for that, none of them having anything to do with the Blain ranch or whatever had happened there.

He realized that most of his worry stemmed from his ignorance about what had happened at the Blain spread. And if ignorance was the problem, maybe it was time to put ignorance aside.

There had to be some kind of law enforcement officer in this little town. There, surely, he could find some information.

McCutcheon got up and began to explore again, looking for some sign of a marshal, a deputy, or a sheriff.

Chapter Five

McCutcheon wandered around another fifteen minutes before he finally spotted what passed for a town marshal's office in this little community.

He approached the door. A CLOSED sign hung crookedly behind the door's dusty window.

McCutcheon was about to turn away, but a subtle motion on the other side of the window made him look more closely. A man was inside the room, seated at a desk.

McCutcheon rapped on the door and received no response. He knocked again, without evoking reaction. So he opened the door himself.

The man who had been lounging back in a chair with his hat over his eyes, almost fell in a mad scramble to come upright, and to grab and hide the whiskey bottle on the desktop before him. He managed to get it under the desk with his right hand, while slapping his hat back into its proper place with his left.

"Hell's bells, friend, don't you know how to knock?" The man had a rusty badge pinned crookedly on the left side of his shirt.

"I did knock," McCutcheon replied, wondering just how early in the day this fellow began drinking. "Sorry if I startled you . . . I thought this was a public office and open to whoever wants to come in."

"Say what, now?"

A drunkard, and half deaf, too.

"Never mind. I just came looking for information."

"What do you want?"

"I need to talk to the town marshal. Would that be you?"

"It's me. So talk and be done with it."

"Do you know of anything unusual going on out at the Abel Blain ranch?"

The marshal's squinting eyes went wide, then suspicion instantly darkened the man's features. "Why are you asking me about that?"

"I've got a personal interest. A friend has been drawn into the situation, and I'd like to know what that situation is so I can know whether he's safe."

"What do you mean, 'drawn into the situation'?"

"It's a complicated story. All I want to know are the basic facts. Did somebody get robbed out there? Shot? Threatened?"

"Listen here—you'd best stay out of that little matter."

"But what *is* that 'little matter?' "

"I know nothing."

"Obviously you know *something.*"

"I hear rumors. And I'd just as soon not hear even those."

"For a law officer, you don't seem too eager to know what's going on around you."

"Look, friend, I'll tell you as straight as I'll tell anybody: This badge counts for very little with me. My brother owns the saloon at the end of the street, and he's given me a piece of that pie. That's where my money comes from, not from this sorry job. The town powers couldn't find nobody else willing to take the sorry job . . . and I'll not take it again once my term is up. Anyway, as regards to the Blain situation, my jurisdiction goes no further than the boundaries of this miserable town. Blain lives beyond them boundaries, and is therefore of as much concern to me as a bucket of spit."

"So you're not going to give me any information at all?" McCutcheon asked.

"I ain't getting involved in no kidnapping, friend. Not no how, no way. And I advise you to stay out of it, too. Once people get wind of ransom money on the move, they can get greedy, and dangerous."

Kidnapping. McCutcheon's mind raced as pieces suddenly fell together.

"Who was kidnapped?" he asked.

"Good day, friend," the marshal said. "I've said all I intend to say."

"How much they pay you for this job, Marshal? However much it is, it's too much."

The lawman smirked, reached beneath the desk, and pulled out the whiskey bottle. "I'll drink to that," he said.

He was tilting back the bottle and draining its contents as McCutcheon pulled the door shut behind him. *Kidnapping. Ransom.*

Once he was out on the street, McCutcheon mulled it over. Somebody at the Blain ranch apparently had been kidnapped, or was under threat of kidnapping . . .

Who? Blain himself was still there. His wife was long dead.

It had to be Bethany Colby, the young beauty he'd seen in that painting. The comments he'd heard earlier about the "poor girl" suddenly made sense.

He sat down on the edge of a boardwalk and stared at a sleeping dog lying in a sunny spot across the street. How would Penn and his undescribed "job" fit into a kidnapping scenario?

It was easy to figure out the likelihood. Kidnappings meant ransom. Penn, and probably those other men he'd talked about, were the deliverers of the ransom. Ransom riders.

What had that whiskey-guzzling marshal just said? *Once people get wind of ransom money on the move, they can get greedy, and dangerous . . .*

McCutcheon came to his feet and headed back toward his hotel on the run.

McCutcheon checked out of his hotel as quickly as possible, then carried his rifle and saddlebagged possessions to the livery, where he paid his fee and recovered his horse and saddle. As quickly as possible, he saddled up and headed out of town, back toward the Blain ranch.

The sky was partly overcast, the clouds pushed by winds, so the sunlight was obscured one moment and allowed to shine through the next. It vanished behind a thick cloudbank just as McCutcheon came into view of the ranch house, crossing the same hillock he and Penn had crested the day before. He hoped the sudden darkness wasn't an omen.

The ranch looked as empty as before. McCutcheon rode down to the house, dismounted, and tied his horse to the fence.

By the time he was done, Will Lincoln had emerged onto the porch, with a Mexican ranch hand beside him. Lincoln wore a pistol and the ranch hand carried a shotgun. There was no friendly manner about him this time.

"Mr. McCutcheon, I believe?" Lincoln said. His hand rested on the butt of his pistol, and McCutcheon noticed that the tie-down thong had been removed. The Mexican, meanwhile, looked ready to raise that shotgun and cut him down at the slightest of provocations.

McCutcheon, taking the direct and daring approach, strode firmly toward both of them.

Lincoln drew his pistol and leveled it.

Chapter Six

"Please, young man, stop right there," Lincoln said.

McCutcheon did stop, but he was coiled tight as a spring, his fists clenched tight. "Where's Penn?"

"Why have you come back here, Mr. McCutcheon? Were you not told to stay away?"

"I want to see Jake Penn."

"Jake Penn isn't here. He's off doing a job for Mr. Blain."

"Yeah. I think I know what that job is."

Just then, Abel Blain, leaning on a cane, appeared on the porch behind Lincoln. "Hello, Mr. McCutcheon," he said. "I'm surprised to see you."

"I would think so," McCutcheon said. "I suppose you didn't think I'd learn that there's been a kidnapping here. Your niece, right?"

Blain said nothing, but seemed to totter on his cane a little, as if startled to hear this.

"You should have known you can't keep such a thing a secret, Mr. Blain," McCutcheon said. "I learned about the kidnapping easily enough over in Black Hill. And if I know, everyone knows."

Blain said, "I think you should come in, Mr. McCutcheon. I was afraid this might happen."

McCutcheon didn't really want to go inside, but he really had no choice, considering the Mexican's shotgun and Lincoln's pistol.

Blain looked weak and tired, his eyes bleary, as he sank back into a mohair-covered chair with a groan. He lay his cane on the floor beside him and stared back at McCutcheon, who declined to sit. Lincoln and the Mexican stood, too, over near the door, still bearing their weapons.

"Tell me what you've heard," Blain said.

"I've heard there's been a kidnapping here," McCutcheon said.

"Where did you hear what you did?"

"From the supposed town marshal at Black Hill. He says he wants nothing to do with it."

"I'm glad to hear that. The man's a drunkard, and I don't want him involved in this matter at all."

"So there *has* been a kidnapping?"

Blain hesitated, then said, "Yes."

"Your niece?"

Blain nodded.

"How long ago?"

"Three nights ago. She vanished without a trace. Then a letter was found. A demand for ransom if ever I was to see her alive again. And a torn-off sleeve from her dress to show me it was real."

"And Jake Penn is carrying the ransom, right?"

"Not alone. There are eight ransom riders in all, now that he's with them, all well armed, dedicated, and trustworthy men."

"Who are they?"

"They're the very best. Mr. Lincoln here would have been among them, their leader, if his joints allowed him to do what he used to. Thus I've turned the leadership of the expedition over to Keith Dresden in his place. Dresden is a good and reliable man."

"Why did you drag Penn into this at all, if you already have good men carrying the ransom?"

"Because I can't think of a man alive who I'd rather have helping me with such an important task as Jake

Penn. Frankly, I could consider it hardly less than a divine sign when he came to me asking for work when the most important job that I'll ever have to see done lay spread before us. With Jake there, I feel all the more sure that the ransom will safely get where it needs to go. And I'll get my Bethany back again."

"How much ransom are you preparing to pay?"

Suspicion tightened Blain's features. "You'll excuse me if I don't answer that."

"Very well. But I won't excuse you if Penn gets hurt, or worse, trying to guard it. I'm sure the ransom is a substantial sum, more than most men could ever hope to come by in honest means, no doubt."

Blain held his silence.

"The word is out, Mr. Blain. People know about the kidnapping. And many of them couldn't care less if you ever get your beloved Bethany back again. Your ransom riders are in great danger."

Blain's hands squeezed into tight fists and began to tremble. "Tell me what you would have had me do differently than what I've done, Mr. McCutcheon. Tell me that . . . and tell me as if it was one of your *own* loved ones at risk! Then you'll see the position I'm in."

"You should have gone to the law. The Texas Rangers, in particular. Let them work with the *federales* and get her back, without endangering eight good men."

"The letter specifically said that any involvement of the Rangers or any other agency of the law, American or Mexican, would result in the immediate death of Bethany. And I believe it."

"Then couldn't the money have been sent in some other form . . . a transfer of funds through bank accounts, something that couldn't be touched?"

"Cash. Those were the terms. Cash in a strongbox.

Anything else, and Bethany would die. There was blood on that dress sleeve, Mr. McCutcheon. *Blood.*"

As he looked at Blain, McCutcheon couldn't help but feel compassion for him. Truly his situation was dire and difficult.

"Mr. Blain, perhaps you did what you had to do. And that being so, perhaps you can understand that there's something I have to do, too. You told me to imagine that I had a loved one out there in danger. Well, I do. Jake Penn has become a closer friend to me than any other human being I've ever known. Right now he's out there carrying you and God-only-knows how much money, with nothing but seven men around him to protect him and a whole world's worth of scoundrels and thieves and murderers who'd gladly try to get that money, and will. So I've got to go after him."

"You can't do that, sir."

"I know you don't want me involved, Mr. Blain, because you don't know me. But I have no choice. Penn is my partner."

"Sir, please, I beg you—don't force this issue. At this point I can't afford anything happening that would endanger Bethany."

"That's already happened. It happened the moment that news of the kidnapping got out."

Blain was a man on the verge of an emotional breakdown and barely holding himself together. He gestured at Will Lincoln, who stepped forward, leveling his pistol.

"Sorry, Mr. McCutcheon. You're going to have to come with us."

McCutcheon reflexively reached toward his own pistol, but stopped his hand in midair. His pistol was tied down; Lincoln's was out and cocked. There was also that Mexican with the shotgun to be considered.

McCutcheon turned to Blain. "You've *got* to let me

go to Penn, Mr. Blain. All I want to do is help him. I'll be the ninth rider."

"No," Blain said. "They'd kill Bethany."

"What do you want me to do with him, Mr. Blain?" Will Lincoln asked. "The lockup?"

"Yes. That's the best."

"Lockup?" McCutcheon said.

"When you're this close to the border, there's a tendency for a lot of Mexican rustlers, thieves, murdering types, and so on, to come over and cause all kinds of problems," Lincoln said. "There's no real jail anywhere near, so we had to make one ourselves to hold men we catch until the Rangers or some other law agents can come along to deal with them."

"You don't have the authority to lock me up!" McCutcheon exclaimed.

"I have the authority of a man who must do all he can to save the life of a young woman who is trapped in a terrifying and dangerous situation," Blain said.

"So I'm to be locked up like a criminal for wanting to help my friend?"

"That's the long and the short of it, Mr. McCutcheon," Lincoln said. "Now come on. Let's get you put away."

McCutcheon walked at gunpoint out of the house and around the side. He eyed his horse, still tied at the fence, and fantasized about making a break for it. Maybe they'd let him ride away.

No. He knew better. If Lincoln hesitated to shoot him, the Mexican wouldn't. It seemed to McCutcheon that the Mexican had a crazed look deep in his eye. The fellow would probably love the chance to blast a gringo with that wicked-looking shotgun of his.

"Mr. Lincoln, let me go. I'll ride away from here. I'll cause no trouble. I promise."

"Sorry, son," Lincoln replied. "I take no pleasure

in treating you this way. Believe me. What I do, I do for Abel, and for Bethany."

"She'll not be rescued at all if that ransom money is stolen before it gets where it's supposed to go," McCutcheon said.

"That's enough from you, young man," Lincoln replied. "Panch, urge him on."

The Mexican prodded the small of McCutcheon's back with the shotgun.

McCutcheon knew he was defeated. Fury briefly swelled inside of him, but dwindled right away to a deflating sense of defeat. He stood while Will Lincoln disarmed him, right down to his pocket knife.

"You'll get all of this back when this is safely over," he said.

McCutcheon was taken to a small, thickly built log hut behind the Blain house, with the chinking between the logs covered over by heavy wood slabs spiked into place. Lincoln pulled a key from his pocket and fumbled with the rusted padlock on the heavy, metal-trimmed door.

"There's candles in a box in the corner, and a few matches. Let me advise you not to try to set the place aflame. You'll only get yourself killed by the smoke before we can get you out."

"This is the sorriest thing I've ever had happen to me," McCutcheon fumed.

The Mexican shoved McCutcheon inside. Lincoln closed the door.

"Hey!" McCutcheon yelled. "Leave the door open at least long enough for me to find the candles!"

"Feel around for them!" Lincoln hollered back as he snapped the padlock closed.

Chapter Seven

Penn rode near the rear of the group of eight, his attention shifting between the Mexican landscape spread around him, the strongbox strapped onto the packsaddle of the horse that trudged along in the midst of the group, and the slumped shoulders of Keith Dresden at the head of the band.

It was quite hard to believe he was actually carrying ransom money into Mexico. This certainly wasn't what he had in mind when he'd come to Abel Blain to find work. But he didn't resent the task. He would do anything for Abel, and for Bethany, who was to Jake Penn like a niece or granddaughter.

He wondered how much money was in that strongbox. Blain hadn't said, but one of the others had whispered something about half a million dollars.

Penn hadn't so much as touched the strongbox, but he'd watched it being loaded and strapped onto the back of the horse. He'd been able to tell it was heavy, so he suspected that at least part of the money it contained was in gold.

Dresden turned and looked back over the group of riders, as he did from time to time. He settled an icy stare on Penn.

"Keeping up there, nappy?" he asked, smirking.

Penn ignored the insulting man and his foolish question. Obviously Penn was keeping up. No one in the group had fallen behind. But when Dresden turned forward again, Penn stared at the back of his head and fantasized briefly about emptying his shotgun into the spot just below Dresden's hat brim. If he did it just right he could send Dresden's head spinning flipping through the air like a well-kicked toy ball.

He enjoyed the mental image of it.

It wouldn't happen. Jake Penn simply didn't have murder in him.

He sighed. It was a frustrating thing sometimes to be virtuous.

A man who had been riding behind Penn pulled up beside him. Penn looked over and got a nod and touch of the hat from Walt Sampson.

"I don't think he likes you much," Sampson said quietly, tipping his head toward Dresden.

"It's pretty evident," said Penn.

"Don't pay him much mind," Sampson said. "He's that way with anybody of your race. There's a lot of folks out there like that, you know."

Penn smiled ever so slightly. "I've come to notice that over the years."

Sampson chuckled. "I suppose you would tend to notice that, a lot more than me. Hey, I hear you're partners with a white fellow."

"That's right. He's a good deal younger than me, but he's a good riding companion. His name's Jim McCutcheon."

"How'd you come to take up with him?"

"He washed over a waterfall inside a log house, and I rescued him."

"No! Really?"

"That's right. Gospel truth."

"And he rides with you out of gratitude?"

"He rides with me mostly because he can't seem to find nothing better to do with his life. So he helps me look for my sister."

"What do you mean?"

"That's what I do: I look for my sister. Her name is Nora, and I ain't seen her since the times we were both slaves. I've been trying to track her down for years. I don't aim to quit until I find her."

"Do you know she's still alive?"

"I have reason to believe she is."

"Is McCutcheon good help in tracking her?"

"He's good companionship, as I said. He's loyal, capable . . . and his folks helped me out many years ago. So I'm glad to have his company."

"Why didn't he come along with you here?"

"Abel didn't want it. He doesn't know Cutch, so he didn't want to take a chance on trusting him with such a job as this, I guess."

"Speaking along those same lines . . . have you considered how much money is in that strongbox, and how much a temptation it would be to a lot of people if word got out about it?"

"I have considered it indeed. I've also considered that these kinds of things generally *do* get out, despite all efforts to keep them quiet."

Sampson nodded. "That's the very reason I didn't want my son involved. His name is Jeff. He works for Abel Blain, like I do. He's a fine cowboy. He and me have become mighty good friends, especially since his mother passed on a few years ago."

"Does he know about the kidnapping?"

"No. Only the eight of us here, and Abel himself, and the hired help at the ranch. Almost all the cowboys, my son Jeff included, had already left for roundup when the kidnapping took place. They never knew. A few of us, including Dresden, were called back from the roundup, but they made up a story to cover up why it was done. Nobody except those who have to know about this, do know about it. If we're lucky."

"If we're lucky," repeated Penn.

They rode a little longer in silence.

"I am sorry for how Dresden acts toward you," Sampson said after a spell. "He's a strange and hateful man sometimes. But he handles his duties well, I'll grant him that. And he's brave. Did you know he actually wanted to carry that ransom all by himself?"

"Is that right?" Penn stared again at Dresden, pondering that intriguing bit of information.

"Yep. Abel wouldn't hear of it, of course. You don't send that much money out with just one man to guard it. But it was bold of Dresden to be willing to do that."

"There might have been something besides bravery that would make a man volunteer to do such a task alone," Penn suggested.

Sampson didn't reply right away. He seemed not to immediately grasp Penn's implication. When he did, though, he quickly jumped to Dresden's defense.

"Oh, no, don't think that! Keith Dresden's an honest man. He has many good qualities despite the bad way he's treated you. If he wasn't honest, Mr. Blain would never have put him in charge and let him read the letter. And I have to say that Dresden has risen to the occasion. These good horses we ride, we can thank him for. All the best mounts on the ranch were out on roundup, you see, but Dresden went and saw his brother who deals in horses over near Black Hill, and obtained these for us."

"A fine thing to do."

"I thought so."

Penn, for his part, was beginning to think that Sampson was one of those occasional men one encountered who were so naturally trusting and goodhearted that they were virtually blind to the treacherous side of human nature. Penn's intuitions about Dresden did not reassure him that the man was so fine and good as Sampson seemed to think.

Penn had to admit, thought, that Dresden's racism made him naturally unlikable, and might be tainting his perceptions of the man's character otherwise.

"Did Dresden tell his brother why he wanted those horses?"

"Others have already asked that same question. He said he told him only that they were needed for roundup."

Penn hoped that was all Dresden had told him. Word about what was really going on wasn't something that needed getting out for any reason or from any source.

"I hope that's all he told him," Penn said.

"Me, too," Sampson replied.

Chapter Eight

The same little Mexican boy who had seen to Penn and McCutcheon's horses had brought McCutcheon his supper about sunset. By that time, McCutcheon had already examined the walls and ceiling of the prison hut, looking for ways to get out.

He'd found none. He might have rushed out past the Mexican boy when he'd brought in the food, if not for the fact the Mexican man with the shotgun was with him. The boy and man looked a lot alike, he noticed. Probably father and son.

Now supper was long past, and McCutcheon's patience was running as low as his candle supply. If they ever came back to pick up the dirty dishes, he'd ask for more candles. But he wasn't sure they were coming back.

He trudged back and forth in the small space. His shadow was large on the wall, and shaking like a nervous ghost as the breeze by his constant pacing made the candle flame flicker.

Blast it all! Was he to be locked up here for days? He hadn't so much as a bed or a slop jar. A dog deserved better than this. Surely they planned to bring him some bedding later on, and offer him a few moments outside to relieve himself.

Blain had no authority to hold him like this. He vowed that when all this was over, he'd see Blain answer to the law for this wrongful imprisonment. This was no better than a kidnapping itself!

McCutcheon made a fast turn, stirring up a stronger breeze than before, and therewith snuffed out the candle. The room was plunged into pitch blackness.

He found the matches and relit the candle. With a sudden curse of frustration, he kicked the wooden box that held the candles. The plates atop it flew into the air and crashed onto the dirt floor. The box itself scooted away from the wall, scraping away some of the dirt.

Dirt floor . . .

Maybe he could dig his way out of here!

He dropped to his knees and felt the floor. It was hard-packed, cool and unrelenting as stone. He clawed at it with his fingernails and was barely able to make a scratch.

Curse the luck! He'd never get out of here. He could never dig through this floor, especially with no tools.

He scooted the box farther away from the wall and sat down on it glumly. He looked down at the area of the wall that previously had been covered by the box.

Something looked different about that portion. He cocked his head and squinted at it, holding the candle close.

It appeared that one section of log might have been cut away at some time, then patched. He got on his knees again and looked closely, pushing and pulling at the patch with his hand.

It seemed to give a little. Encouraged, he worked harder. He strained and labored until sweat began to bead on his forehead.

Soon enough, however, he saw that his labors would do no good. Whoever had patched the section had done a good job. It was almost as solid as the rest of the wall.

Suddenly, the lock rattled. Someone was at the door.

McCutcheon got up and scooted the box back in place. Abruptly he decided that when that door opened, he'd make a run for it. Run right over that Mexican boy and take his chances that the shotgun-toter wasn't there this time, or might be too rattled to actually shoot.

When the door opened, however, the figure that was revealed was not that of the boy. This was a man.

"You in there, friend?"

McCutcheon hadn't heard this voice before, he didn't think.

"I'm here. Who are you?"

"My name's Jeff Sampson."

"Am I supposed to know you?"

"No, but I think we've got the same interest. If you want to go after those ransom riders, then come on. We've got a lot of traveling ahead of us."

The man was speaking softly, obviously concerned about being detected.

"How'd you get the key to that lock?" McCutcheon asked, wondering if this was a setup designed to get him shot as a runaway.

"I stole it from the house. And almost got caught at it. I'll explain all this later—right now we've got to move fast." The man sounded young, younger than McCutcheon himself.

"What about my weapons? My horse?"

"All waiting for you. Hurry!"

McCutcheon didn't have to be told another time. He left the hut and followed the stranger through the darkness.

Chapter Nine

The Gajardo Mission showed plenty of signs of frequent occupancy—old campfires, assorted refuse strewn about, horse droppings, tracks in abundance—but none of continuing use. The mission consisted solely of a few stone walls, a high tower jutting into the dark sky, and empty buildings with windows like dark and staring eyes.

Only the campfire that Jimmy Couch and Alan Doelin had built brightened the scene. In the half-globe of light that it cast, seven of the eight ransom riders huddled for warmth and food and a sense of separation from the darkness beyond.

Dresden, though, stood at the arch-topped gate in the mission wall, staring out across the plains and waiting.

From somewhere out there, the message would come, if all went according to what was said in the ransom letter. Someone would contact them at this place and tell them where to convey the money.

Perhaps the kidnappers would go ahead and take the money right here, but Penn doubted it. Had they revealed in the ransom letter exactly where they would be, and when, it would have been an invitation for Blain to make arrangements for officers of either American or Mexican law, or both, to intercept them at this point. The logic of this criminal venture demanded that the ransom delivery be in two stages, the first simply to get the money well away from the ranch, the second to convey it to its final place of exchange.

The information would probably come by means of one, maybe two messengers. Maybe not even actual members of the kidnapping band, whoever they were, but simply hired men. There was much quiet speculation about this among the men encircling the fire, and a sense of eagerness to see how close their predictions came to the reality. No one really knew what to expect. None of this group, except for Dresden, had read the ransom letter.

Every man was weary, Penn especially, but no one was willing to sleep just yet.

"I'd like to know how the kidnapping happened," Penn asked Walt Sampson.

"Nobody knows exactly what happened," he said. "As I hear it, Miss Colby made a private journey to Black Hill, something she did from time to time, with no one worried about it because there seemed no danger. She left on Monday morning and was to return that night.

"She didn't return, though. Mind you, this is all how it was told to us, for all of us here had already gone out on roundup at that point. Anyway, when she didn't come back, Mr. Blain sent out some of the people still about the ranch to look for her. But there was no sign of anything.

"The next morning, though, some evidence was found that there might have been a struggle of some sort about halfway out the road between the ranch and Black Hill. But there was nothing all that clear, no trail that could be followed.

"That night, Tuesday night, a packet was found at the edge of the ranch grounds. It contained a letter written to Mr. Blain, and a torn-off sleeve of Miss Colby's dress. Nobody read the letter except for Mr.

Blain, and later, Dresden. But it outlined what was to be done if Miss Colby was to be seen alive again.

"The next morning, riders were sent out to fetch those of us here back from roundup. No explanation was given other than that Mr. Blain needed us. The other cowboys—my son being one of them—were to remain on roundup as before.

"We came back and learned what had happened. Mr. Blain asked us all to be the ones to carry the ransom, and we agreed. Dresden was ready to carry the ransom all alone. He tried hard to persuade Mr. Blain to let him do it, but there was nothing doing on that. Mr. Blain figured no one man would be safe, carrying a large amount of money all alone. And I suppose it was also to help make sure nobody could be ever accused of taking the money for themselves, you know.

"Anyhow, we all agreed to help out. Then you came along and joined us, and now here we are."

"Somebody's out there," Dresden suddenly called over from the arched entranceway.

Some of the men around the fire, not including Penn, came to their feet.

"For God's sake, sit down!" Dresden barked. "I don't want nobody acting spooked or funny in any way."

The men sat down, chagrined.

"I don't see nothing out there," Leroy Shepard said.

Doelin allowed as how he hadn't, either.

"That's because you've been looking into the flames," Penn replied. "It's not something you should do at a time like this. You'll see nothing but spots for more than a minute. I always avoid staring into a fire."

"Well, what do *you* see then, sharp-eyes?" Doelin countered defensively.

"I see a rider approaching," Penn replied. "One man, barely visible to me. Coming in slowly with a

poncho across his shoulders. Broad hat. I can barely
make out the lines of him and his horse against the
sky. He's at the top of that little rise . . . now he's
coming on across. Too dark to make him out against
the background now."

"Could you tell if he was carrying arms?"

"I'd wager he's got something hid under that poncho. Sawed-off shotgun, maybe?"

"I can see him now!" Michael Klugan, the youngest
of the ransom riders, chimed in.

The others could as well at this point. The man had
ridden in close to the arch-topped gate.

Though nothing of his features could be made out
because of the darkness, the newcomer had an ominous quality about him, like the reaper of death himself, riding in to call on the living. Or one of the
Horsemen of the Apocalypse, maybe. Bethany Colby's
apocalypse, anyway.

"Howdy!" the horseman called. His voice was inor-
dinately cheerful and light, playing counterpoint to
that vague but fearsome visual image he presented.
The contrast between his voice and image only contributed to his ominous aura.

"Howdy yourself," Dresden called back. "Are you
the man we've been expecting?"

"Well, you know, I believe I probably am," the man
replied. His voice was that of a Southerner. Alabama,
possibly. He sounded like he was smiling as he spoke,
and Penn had the mental impression, for some reason,
of a wide mouth with overly large teeth.

"I'm coming out to see you," Dresden said.

"Very friendly of you," the man called back.

Dresden strode out toward the rider, who did not
dismount his horse. Dresden was unarmed, but every
man there, Penn included, stood ready to defend him
if trouble should come.

There were no handshakes. Dresden and the rider

engaged in conversation. They were too far away for their voices to be heard.

The rider handed something to Dresden, who examined it briefly. They talked some more.

At last Dresden turned and walked back toward the mission. The rider, meanwhile, turned his mount and vanished into the darkness.

Penn let out his breath. He'd been holding it for the last twenty seconds without even realizing it.

"What's the word?" Shepard asked.

"We've got to carry the ransom to Castillo," Dresden said.

"Somehow I figured it might come to that," Doelin said. "Murder, kidnapping, thieving . . . follow the stench of any of them in these parts, and they'll lead you to Castillo."

"Yes, and that's bad news," Shepard said.

"What do you mean?" Klugan asked.

"Ever heard of the Gajardo Canyon, young man?" Shepard said.

"Yes. What about it?"

"To get to Castillo, we'll have to go through it. It's the only way through the mountains."

"What's bad about that?"

"There's the fact that the place has rockslides about every other day. In the last five, six years alone, I've heard of three people who got killed there by falling rocks. Either flattened or conked on the noggin by boulders about the size of your backside," Shepard replied. "But what worries me most in this situation is that the Gajardo Canyon is one of the primest spots for an ambush that I can think of."

A couple of others grunted agreement.

"There's no reason for us to be ambushed," Dresden said, with—oddly, Penn thought—a defensive tone. "We're delivering the ransom right into their hands! Why would they need to try to take it?"

Walt Sampson spoke. "It's not the kidnappers themselves we have to worry about. It's others who might have learned what's going on. A lot of people would try hard to get their hands on the amount of money in that box . . . and the canyon is the best place I could think of to try to do it."

Chapter Ten

Dresden seemed very unhappy to hear Sampson's comment.

"Nobody knows about this kidnapping, or this ransom, but us," Dresden said sharply. "*Nobody*. I made sure word didn't get out."

Penn wondered how the man could be so confident. Perhaps he was personally careful not to let information slip, but how could he know others hadn't? There were quite a few employees on the Blain ranch. No doubt they had friends and family members. No doubt some had loose lips.

Jimmy Couch said, "I don't know why you're only just now growing concerned about that canyon. No matter where we might have been told to take the ransom, we'd have had to pass through Gajardo Canyon."

"He's right," Dresden said. "So our situation isn't made any worse by this. We have to go through that canyon anyway. So let's just get it done, get that money delivered, and get the young lady back safe again."

Penn said, "Ain't it going to be easy for most anybody, then, to figure out that we'll have to go through that canyon?"

"He's got a point," Shepard said.

"Nobody's going to figure it out because nobody *knows* about this but us," Dresden said. He faced

Penn. "Listen to me, darky: I've made no secret of the fact I don't want you here. I don't know you, don't trust you, and don't like your kind. But because Abel Blain wanted you here, I've abided you. But I'll not do so if you start flapping that mouth and trying to stir up worries."

Penn stared directly into Dresden's eyes. "The time may come when you and I have a very intense personal discussion of some of these problems you seem to have with me."

Dresden's brows rose and he stepped back, grinning. "Did you hear this African? Why, he can talk like an educated man! 'Intense personal discussion!' You ever hear such as that?"

"We've got enough to worry about without this nonsense, Keith," Sampson said to Dresden.

"I don't want to go through that canyon," Klugan said. "I got a bad feeling about it. We need to find another way."

Dresden wheeled on him this time. "There *ain't* no other way! Hell! I knew you were too young to be brought along, Klugan. You ain't going to coward out of this now." Dresden shook his head. "Boys and darkies! We'll be lucky to make this work at all."

"I think Klugan's right. I don't think we should go through that canyon," Penn said.

"I told you: There *is* no other way, damn it!" Dresden shot back.

"Mountains can be climbed and crossed."

"He might have a point there, Keith," Shepard said. "It would be difficult, but we could make it over the mountains if we had to. We could deliver that ransom without having to risk ambush. You can't really know that word about this hasn't gotten out. News like this generally does."

Dresden shook his head firmly. "The kidnappers are watching our route. They expect us to pass through the canyon. If we go some other way, they'll think something's wrong. They'll kill the girl."

"That rider told you they'll be watching the canyon?"

"He did."

Penn wondered if this was true. But there was no way to know. Nobody else had been able to hear what was said between Dresden and the messenger.

"What was it that man handed you?" Couch asked.

Dresden held out a woman's dress sleeve. "It matches the one that was left with the ransom letter. There's no question that they've got her. Now, gentlemen, boys, and darkies, this little revival meeting is at an end. We're going through the canyon after first light. Meanwhile, I suggest we try to get some sleep while we can. I'll stand guard. For some reason I'm not feeling particularly tired just now."

McCutcheon found it an odd feeling, riding along through the night with a stranger who had just rescued him from confinement for reasons he couldn't quite figure out. He'd asked Jeff Sampson to explain himself, but so far Sampson had begged off. "Let's ride, not talk," he'd said. "I want to put as many miles behind us as we can."

Once on the other side of the Rio Grande, McCutcheon halted his horse.

Jeff Sampson did the same, turning. "Why are you stopping?"

"Because I'll go no farther without understanding what's going on."

"I told you what's going on. We're going after the ransom riders. To join them and help protect that ransom. To make sure it gets where it is supposed to go, so Bethany . . . so Miss Colby will be safe."

"This is all a little too odd for me. Tell me how you found out about the kidnapping. And how you

managed to get back here, get me loose, and get all
my possessions back at the same time."

"Can't I explain this later?"

"No. Now."

Jeff Sampson sighed. "All right. Horses need a rest,
anyway, I guess."

They dismounted. Sampson paced about as he
talked.

"We were on roundup . . . then some men showed
up from the ranch, to call some of us back. My father
was one of those called back. Seven of them in all
returned to the ranch. No reason was given, and they
tried to make it out like it was nothing important. But
you could tell it was. They don't call men back like
that for nothing.

"I asked Pap straight out why they were going back,
but he said he didn't know. Maybe he really didn't.
Anyway, I had a feeling about it. Something was
wrong. But I couldn't guess what.

"The next day, Curly Jackson, one of our number,
got pulled off his horse while roping a bullock. Nearly
broke his leg. They sent me with him over to a town
that was a few miles away where there was a doctor.

"While Curly was getting tended, I walked around
town a little. In a barroom I heard men talking about
the Blain ranch. There was mention of a kidnapping,
and of Bethany Colby. It got my attention right off. I
asked questions. There weren't many answers, but
there were sure rumors aplenty, and they scared me
to death. They were saying that Miss Colby had been
kidnapped into Mexico, and there was to be a big
ransom paid by Abel Blain to get her back."

McCutcheon asked, "How had the news gotten
out?"

"There's all kinds of folks who work at the ranch.
People come and go, and people talk. Once news of
something like that gets out, it spreads like fire in dry

grass. And you never know who might have planned such a kidnapping. Maybe somebody talked it up even before it happened."

"So what did you do?"

"I left Curly abandoned there in that town. I had no other choice. I realized why Pap and the others had been called back. They were going to carry the ransom. And it came to my mind that if they had a big amount of money, being carried into Mexico, and if news of the kidnapping had already spread, as it had . . . you can figure the rest."

"I already have," McCutcheon said. "It's the same reason I came back to the ranch. My friend Jake Penn is one of the ransom bearers, just like your father. I'm determined to find out where the ransom is being taken, and to follow and help them out."

Jeff nodded and went on. "Before I got back to the ranch, I'd had time to think things through. I realized that they were trying to keep the kidnapping secret. Otherwise they'd have told us all straight out why the seven were called back. It came to mind that it might be best not to show myself at the ranch right away, to maybe talk to Panch, if I could, and see what was going on."

"Panch . . . that's the Mexican who seemed ready to shotgun me if he got half a chance."

Jeff shook his head. "You misread him, though it's no surprise. Panch does what he's told, and they'd told him to guard you. Anyway, to make a long story short, I did manage to talk to Panch when I got back to the ranch, without anyone else knowing I'd come back at all. He told me the whole story of the kidnapping. And he told me about you and your partner showing up. He said you'd come back to the ranch from Black Hill because word was out about the kidnapping. He told me you wanted to go to help guard the ransom

because of your partner, but that Mr. Blain had locked
you up.

"I thought to myself: This McCutcheon fellow and
myself are surely thinking along the same lines. I decided that maybe we should team up together. Two
heads—and two guns—are better than one.

"Panch was willing to help me break you free. He
admitted to me that he was as worried as you and me
were about the fact the kidnapping was no longer a
secret. He gave me the key to the lockup house, got
your horse, saddle, your guns . . . and now, here we
are."

McCutcheon said, "I'll be! I reckon I *did* misread
that Mexican."

"Like I said, Panch does what he's told. But he also
is his own man. He helped lock you up, but he didn't
agree with it. He was ready to come with us himself,
as a matter of fact, but I talked him out of it. This
isn't the kind of job he's got the skills to do. And his
son has no mother alive. If something happened to
Panch, Pablo would be left alone."

"Will Panch be in trouble with Blain for busting
me out?"

"He'll say you managed to break out on your own.
He'll claim he forgot to close the padlock and you
were able to jiggle it off the latch from the inside.
Well, now you've heard my story. Are you still with
me?"

"You know I am. But where exactly are we going?"

"Panch said that the ransom riders were to go to the
Gajardo Mission and await word from the kidnappers.
Beyond that, he doesn't know. I don't suppose anyone
knows, not until the kidnappers give further direction."

"Where's the Gajardo Mission?"

"Still well ahead. We've got a lot of riding to do."

"What if the ransom riders won't accept our help?"

"They've got no choice. I'll not have my father in such danger without me being by his side. I don't care what he or anybody else thinks about it. Besides, I want to make absolutely sure that Bethany gets back safe. That matters more than anything."

A flash of insight came to McCutcheon. "She's your lady, isn't she?"

Jeff Sampson looked away; McCutcheon had the sense he was embarrassed. "I don't know that she's even all that aware I'm alive. But I think she's a fine lady, and I wish she would just . . . I don't know. Give me a chance."

McCutcheon nodded. "I've been right where you are, my friend. More than once. Come on, let's ride. We'll make sure she comes back safe and sound, Jeff. And your father and Penn, too."

Chapter Eleven

The mountains loomed before the band of ransom bearers, rocky and imposing, cutting off the view of all that lay beyond.

The only visible route through those mountains lay before them, a jagged cut in the land. The trail that had led them here was no true road, but it was well worn, as people, like free-roaming livestock, tend to find and repeatedly use the easiest routes through or around obstacles. Generations of people had traveled the Gajardo Canyon trail and had beaten it deep into the northern Mexico soil.

The ransom riders paused as a group at the head of the trail, which descended at a relatively steep angle into the shadowed canyon. A hundred yards ahead, the trail made a turn that followed the canyon's natural curve. Thus most of the way ahead of them remained unseen, and Penn didn't like the feeling that gave him.

He studied the sides of the canyon. Jutting, massive rocks, sheer cliffs, pockmarked with recesses and caves, with plenty of natural crevices.

Indeed, this was a natural ambush site.

He noticed, too, the heavy evidence of rockslides. This canyon seemed to be doing its best to broaden its own top and fill in its own base. Slopes of fragmented rock and shattered boulders strewn in various tormented patterns at the base of the cliffs from which they'd fallen gave the canyon the appearance of an obstacle course. The trail through the canyon's base was a rather fluid one, taking a new route every time the canyon walls belched down a new obstruction.

Penn studied the mountains. Might it be possible to cross them and avoid this uninviting canyon altogether? Frankly, it looked nearly impossible. And as much as he didn't like to admit it, he couldn't counter Dresden's claim that deviating from the original plan could result in bad things for Bethany Colby.

Like it or not, it appeared they would indeed have to traverse that canyon, just as Dresden had said. Penn dreaded it thoroughly.

Dresden got down off his horse and made sure the strongbox was adequately strapped in place. "Wouldn't want it to shake loose on this rough trail," he said.

As Dresden worked with the straps, cinching the box more firmly into place, Walt Sampson rode up beside Penn.

"You know," he said softly, "for some reason today, and despite all the defending things I said about him, I just don't feel a lot of trust in that man."

"Neither do I," Penn replied.

Sampson said, "Ah, lawdy! A man can't go by feelings alone, though, can he? Especially at such a time as this. Abel Blain trusts him, and he's always been a better judge of character than me." He pulled his horse forward, ahead of Penn.

Dresden finished his work and remounted his horse. "Let's put this canyon behind us," he said.

Doelin said, "Keith, just in case there is trouble, and something should happen to you, don't you think you ought to tell us where in Castillo that money is to be taken, and who we're supposed to meet, and how?"

"Nothing's going to happen in this canyon," Dresden replied. "We're going to ride through it and come out the other side, and that's that. And it's best that only one of us knows. A man can't betray information he doesn't have."

Penn found this to be suspicious logic. But he kept his mouth shut, somewhat against his own better instincts.

They rode forward, down deeper into the canyon's shadowed base.

Penn could not tell where the first shot came from. He heard it simultaneously with seeing young Michael Klugan contort in a strange, spastic motion, followed by a faint grunt barely audible amid the echoing away of the gunshot. Suddenly there was blood on Klugan, flooding down his left side. He looked at it, then fell from his horse, slowly.

Penn could tell at a glance that he was dead.

Klugan's horse ran off, down the canyon.

"Ambush!" Alan Doelin yelled, his voice raising high in panic. "They're shooting at us from—"

He never finished his sentence. A bullet traveling at a sharp downward angle punched a hole through the front brim of his hat and entered his torso just above the breastbone. He was dead before his body hit the ground. His horse ran off after Klugan's, but Doelin's foot remained hooked into the stirrup. His corpse was dragged about fifty feet over the rocky trail before finally pulling loose.

All was chaos. Gunshots poured down from both sides of the canyon, raining lead in a deadly storm. Penn's horse whinnied and fell, shot through the head. He tumbled off to the left, which probably saved his life in that three slugs hammered the ground in the area where he would have been had his horse stayed upright.

Penn lost his shotgun, but quickly regained it, came to his feet, and scrambled for cover. From the corner of his eye he saw Leroy Shepard go down. Wounded, not killed. Shepard got up, his left arm bleeding and hanging limp, and made for the base of the canyon's northwest side. A bullet hit him in the right knee and made him pitch forward, face-down. Another slug struck him in the center of his back and ended his life.

Jimmy Couch was screaming, running, and firing his pistol wildly into the air with no chance of actually hitting any of the ambushers. Bullets whined off of the rock all around him, but Couch was not struck.

Penn, armed with a shotgun, wished now that he had his rifle. He found momentary cover beneath a ledge that protected him from fire from those directly above him, but which left him exposed from some angles to gunfire from across the canyon, and from the deadly ricochets buzzing all around.

Penn looked out and up, and fired off one barrel at a man drawing a bead on Mark Bradshall, a wide-faced, shy cowboy from whom Penn had not heard more than three words the entire journey. The shot dispersed in a wide pattern and was not sufficiently concentrated to be fatal to the ambusher, but it did cause him to drop his rifle and scream, his hands clasping his face. He held that posture a moment, and Penn pulled out his pistol, took careful aim, and shot the man through the chest.

As best Penn could tell, his was the first successful answer to the ambushers. But it hardly mattered. The ambushers still outnumbered those in the canyon, and were much more safely positioned.

Penn caught a glimpse of another ambusher, moving along the rim of the canyon. He took aim, fired, and saw the man jump wildly as a spray of buckshot struck the side of his body from knee to shoulder. He staggered back, away from the canyon rim, then bumped a boulder and fell back the other way. With a howl he plunged over the edge and fell unmoving on the jagged rocks below.

Another one down.

Penn fired a couple of quick pistol shots at more of their attackers, without results, then reloaded the shotgun.

He heard someone scream nearby, and turned to see Bradshall fall, bleeding badly. Penn was about to scramble out to pull him back under the ledge when Bradshall took another slug through the chest, then a third through the temple.

Penn looked to his left, and saw something that astonished him. Dresden was still astride his horse, moving down the canon, leading the packhorse that carried the strongbox.

And none of the ambushers were shooting at him.

Penn put it all together quickly, and it infuriated him. He raised his pistol, aimed it at Dresden, and fired.

He missed. Dresden kept moving, though taken aback by Penn's shot, which sang past his ear.

Didn't expect anybody to shoot at you, did you, Dresden! Wasn't part of the plan, was it! Penn thought, then he fired again. This time the bullet was not aimed at Dresden, but at the packhorse. This one struck home, and the horse fell. The strongbox broke loose from its ties and tumbled onto the ground but did not break open.

Through the cacophony of gunfire, Penn heard Dresden swear loudly.

Penn caught movement above him, and looked up to see a man scrambling along, trying to find a firing position. Penn raised his pistol and readied to fire as the man looked at him.

Penn froze, taken aback by the sight of the man's face. Penn swiveled his head back toward Dresden, a confused look on his face. Dresden had just disappeared beyond an overhang. In the time that Penn turned back to peer at the ambusher above him, the man found opportunity to pull back, out of sight.

A human figure burst into the area under the ledge, beside Penn. Startled, Penn turned and was about to shoot, but saw that it was Couch. He was bleeding from at least two wounds, but still fighting. His face was white as milk.

"They've killed almost everybody . . . but I don't know about Dresden. Where's Dresden? And where's Walt Sampson?"

There was no time for Penn to answer. Fresh gunfire erupted from across the canyon, bullets whizzing all around them.

The ambushers had found new positions, and were now firing unimpeded into the very space Penn and Couch occupied.

There was nowhere to run but out, no place to be except in the open, and probably nothing to do but die.

If so, Penn decided, he'd die fighting, not hiding. He heard Jimmy Couch grunt and watched him pitch forward, dead.

Penn let out a roar of fury and came out from beneath the ledge, his shotgun blasting.

Chapter Twelve

"They've been here, sure enough," McCutcheon said. "See the tracks?"

He was kneeling just outside the arched doorway of the empty Gajardo Mission. Jeff Sampson was beside him.

"Been here, but gone," Sampson said. "I suppose they must have made their contact with the kidnappers, then."

"Yes. Unfortunately, we don't know where they've gone," McCutcheon replied.

"Well . . . maybe we do," Sampson replied. "Assuming they're taking the money deeper into Mexico, from this point they'd about have to go through the Gajardo Canyon, no matter where they were headed. If I had to take a guess, I'd figure they were going to Castillo. Everything bad that happens here, rustling, murder, theft, whatever, always seems to have its roots in Castillo."

"Which way to Castillo?"

Sampson pointed.

McCutcheon studied the tracks. "Well, it looks like they did head that way. I say let's go after them. Maybe we can catch up."

Sampson was agreeable. Though both young men were tired, they were also energized, sensing that they were at least closing the gap on the ransom riders. They mounted their horses and began to ride.

"Hear that?" Sampson said suddenly.

"What?"

"I thought I heard gunfire way off ahead."

McCutcheon listened but could hear nothing. The wind was shifty today, changing directions often. It could have been that Sampson had picked up something that was audible only for a moment, and with the wind blowing at just the right direction.

"I hope there's not trouble for the ransom riders," McCutcheon said.

"Maybe it was nothing," Sampson said. "But if it was . . . it sounded to me like it was coming from the direction of the Gajardo Canyon."

They rode silently from that point on, with a heightened sense of urgency.

McCutcheon spotted the three riders first.

They were obscured initially by brush along a stream but rode out and into open view just as McCutcheon was about to draw Sampson's attention to them. Sampson drew in his breath when he caught sight of them.

They were big, burly gringos, dirty and unshaven, smiling but not friendly. They wore sidearms with the ties loosened, and had rifles in their saddle boots. As they neared, McCutcheon could smell the odors of tobacco, dirt, and sweat that pervaded their bodies.

"Good day to you, young man," the biggest of the three said.

"Good day," McCutcheon replied. He allowed his horse to turn slightly, trying to make it appear as if it had done so of its own accord. Meanwhile, he slipped off the tie-down string from his own pistol. Every instinct in him told him these men were trouble.

"You fellows might be the ones we're looking for," the man said.

"I doubt it," Sampson said.

"Well, answer me this: Are you the ones bearing the ransom money to be paid for that kidnapped gal from the Blain ranch over in Texas?"

"Not us," Sampson said. "I don't believe we've even heard about that. What kidnapping?"

"Let's search 'em," another of the three said. He had wild, overeager eyes, and licked his lips a lot. The lust for gold was so strong on him you could see it, and that made him dangerous, which is why he was the one McCutcheon chose to aim at as he pulled his pistol free and brought it up.

"What the devil's this?" the center rider said, looking deeply surprised and maybe hurt at being treated so rudely. "Why are you drawing your pistol?"

"Hell, I'll draw mine, too," said the third rider. And he did, remarkably fast, and had it leveled at McCutcheon in less than a second.

But Sampson, in the meantime, had done the same. And there they sat, McCutcheon and Sampson with pistols leveled on the three riders, and one of the riders with a pistol leveled back at them.

The center rider shifted in his saddle a little, and McCutcheon thought he was about to produce his own pistol. He aimed his gun between the man's eyes.

"I wouldn't," he said.

"Just shifting my rump about, that's all. I got a bad case of the piles. It's a tragedy when a man can't live at peace with his own hindquarters, ain't it?" The fellow smiled fulsomely. "Come on, now. Put them pistols down. There's no call for you two getting killed. Just let us have that ransom and we'll send you on your way."

"We got no ransom," McCutcheon said. "Have your partner there put away that pistol, or I'll shoot you. Don't think I'm bluffing."

"Maybe he'll shoot you first," the man said.

McCutcheon aimed at the pistoleer and fired. The

slug, as intended, ripped through the outer part of the man's right shoulder. He dropped his own pistol as if it were red-hot, and groped at his wound.

"Damnation!" he bellowed.

"Next time I'll aim more carefully," McCutcheon said. "I don't always hit a man between the eyes on the first try. Now, all of you, drop your weapons."

"The hell you say!" the one on the left side said.

The center rider, however, lifted a hand in a peacemaking gesture. "Let's hold on here, gentlemen," he said. "This is getting out of hand."

"Drop the weapons, or I'll drop you."

Reluctantly, the would-be highwaymen complied.

"You," McCutcheon said, speaking to the man he'd wounded, "get down off your horse and carry those weapons over to the stream there. Throw them in."

"How am I supposed to carry them? You shot me! I can't even move my arm!"

"You got one good arm left. And you're less likely than the others to try something foolish. Do it! Now!"

It took about three minutes of effort for the wounded man to complete his task. McCutcheon and the center rider held each other's stares throughout the entire time.

When the weapons were dumped, McCutcheon spoke. "Listen to me. We have no ransom. We've got no money to speak of at all, and nothing worth robbing. But we'll kill you right off if you ever show your faces to us again."

The center rider said, "That might be a risk we'll have to take. That's one big ransom, we've heard."

"I told you: We have no ransom. We don't even know what you're taking about."

"We ain't the only ones who know about that kidnapping, my friends," the man said. "Just thought you'd like to know that the word has spread far and wide. There was ranch hands of Blain's talking about it as soon as it happened. You'll never succeed in getting that ransom wherever it's going. Too many people are after it."

"Off your horses. Take off the saddles," McCutcheon demanded.

"Let us go. We'll bother you no more."

McCutcheon fired a shot just to the right of the center rider's ear.

"The saddles," he said.

The riders dismounted and obeyed. The wounded one required help from his companions.

"Carry the saddles over and dump them in the water, too," McCutcheon said.

Curses and protests arose. McCutcheon made a show of readying to kill the leader of the three, which quieted the complaints instantly.

"We'll take your horses," he said. "Fair compensation for the trouble and the threats. If you come after them, we'll kill you."

"This is a hellacious thing to do to a man!" the leader said.

"You were ready to rob us. You've got nothing you can say. Now get those saddles in the water. And while you're over there, take off your boots and throw them in the creek, too."

"And the pants," Sampson contributed.

"Good idea," McCutcheon said. "The pants too."

The men didn't even bother to protest this time. McCutcheon found it hard not to laugh at them. He'd never seen a more poorly executed robbery attempt. These men had made quite a miscalculation, failing to see that a mere superiority of numbers was no match for superiority of intelligence and quickness of wit . . . not to mention draw.

"Start walking," McCutcheon said. "Don't even turn around, and don't make a peep. You do, and I'll come back and put you under snakes."

The trio obeyed, walking gingerly in their stocking-covered feet across the rough land, their ragged long-johns drooping from their bodies and their shirttails dangling.

"Lucky for us they were such fools," Sampson said. "Otherwise they'd have killed us."

"The next ones may not be so foolish," McCutcheon said. "We were lucky this time. Think about it, Jeff: We don't even have the ransom, and still came nigh to getting killed over it. You can figure it's that much worse for the real ransom riders. This is a dangerous game."

"Let's move on," Sampson said. "I'm eager to see that my father is all right."

Chapter Thirteen

But Walt Sampson was not all right.

Weak, bleeding, and struggling to keep his mind from drifting off into delirium and his body from yielding to shock, he staggered across the barren landscape while his life slowly drained away.

He didn't know where he was going, or why. He was simply trying to put as much distance between himself and the Gajardo Canyon as possible. He was fleeing it like a man feeling hell, for hell it had been.

He'd lost his hat, and the sun glaring down was searing his ruddy, easily burned skin. He knew he would not live, and struggled to pray. He did not want to die, and feared what lay beyond it.

"Dear Lord," he whispered. "Dear Lord, save me, and . . . just save me, Lord . . ." It was the only prayer he could come up with. He'd never been a religious man, but wished now that he had been.

Something up ahead was moving. Two men, on horseback, leading three other horses behind them.

He stumbled on a stone and fell to his knees. There he remained, somehow managing to stay upright long enough to see that one of the two riders was his own son. He laughed. An illusion, he was sure. A dying man's hallucination. If so, he welcome it.

"Jeff . . ." he whispered. "Jeff . . . son, I'm shot. I'm done for."

Jeff Sampson was off his horse, running toward him.

The hands that touched Walt were not those of a phantom. It really was Jeff. Walt did not have the strength to wonder how he happened to be here, or why.

"Dear God, Pap! What's happened?"

"Ambushed . . . Gajardo Canyon . . . kidnappers in the rocks above . . . gunned us down . . ."

McCutcheon, now also out of the saddle and at Walt Sampson's side, felt his stomach rise to somewhere just under his throat.

Penn . . .

"How bad are you shot, Pap?"

"Bad . . . bad . . . dying. I'm dying, son."

"No, Pap. No. I won't let you do that. Lie down. Let me tend to you."

"Don't go . . . up there. Don't go to the canyon. Death . . . Surely lies there."

McCutcheon said, "Sir, are there any yet alive?"

"No . . . all dead. All dead."

"You saw it? You saw all of them die?"

"I saw . . . many dead men . . . The kidnappers ambushed us. Gunned us down . . . from the rocks above . . . I want to lie down now, son."

"Pap, I'll get you help. A doctor. We'll get you patched up." Jeff Sampson was speaking through tears.

"Where's your mama, son?" Sampson's mind was going now, ebbing away like his lifeblood. "I ain't seen her in a while. Where's she been?"

"Pap, tell me one thing—did they let Bethany go?"

"Don't know . . . son . . . send your mama up . . . when she comes in." He was talking out of his head now, his present reality fusing with memories.

"I'm going for help, Pap. I'll be back soon. Jim McCutcheon here will stay with you."

"I'm . . . thirsty. Really thirsty."

Jeff Sampson ran to his horse and got a canteen.

When he returned and knelt, he put it to his father's lips.

McCutcheon could have told him that it was too late, for he'd seen the light depart from Walt Sampson's eyes while Jeff was fetching the canteen. But instinct told him it was best if Jeff discovered the truth for himself.

Jeff held his father's head in his lap for a couple of minutes. McCutcheon said nothing, not intruding into the other's privacy.

"He was a good man," Jeff said at last. "I'm glad he was my father."

"I wish I could have known him," McCutcheon said. "You'll take him back to the ranch now, I suppose?"

Jeff, still looking at his father's face, said, "No. I'll bury him here, for now. I've got to go on and make sure Bethany is safe. Then, later, I'll bury him proper."

"And I've got to go see what happened to Jake."

"He said they were all killed, Jim. I'm sorry."

"I've got to see for myself. You understand."

"Yeah. I do."

"We got anything to dig a hole with, Jeff?"

"Just a little camp shovel in my saddlebag."

"We'll work in shifts. I'll dig first."

There was no sign of life in the canyon, but there was abundant evidence of death.

McCutcheon eyed the vultures circling high above, then lowered his eyes to the canyon floor below where dead men lay, and wondered if the vultures had already begun their work.

He wondered, as well, if one of the dead ones below was Penn.

There was only one way to know.

"I suppose it's safe to go down there now," Mc-

Cutcheon said. "The ransom is probably taken by now."

Jeff Sampson, his eyes still red from weeping, replied, "I've been wondering something, Jim. Why did they do this? Why not just take the ransom and be gone? Why did they have to murder them all?"

"I don't know. Maybe they didn't want anyone alive who could identify them."

Sampson paused. "In that case, they'll have killed Bethany, too."

"I suppose so." McCutcheon screwed up his courage. "Well, we got to go down there. But I dread what we might find."

They debated for ten minutes whether to go down on horseback or on foot. The former would allow quicker escape if whoever had done this was still about. The latter, though, would allow them more stealth, and the chance to perhaps not be detected at all.

The factor that clinched the decision was the realization that the dead men below had been on horseback, and it obviously had done them no good at all.

They hid their horses in a thicket well back from the canyon's entrance, then took their weapons and advanced, full of dread, toward the canyon's mouth.

PART II

Castillo

Chapter Fourteen

McCutcheon leaned against a boulder, staring at a bit of scrub brush on the ground ahead of him as if it was an intensely fascinating object, being far too preoccupied with trying not to become sick to his stomach.

So far he was doing better than Jeff Sampson, who had already heaved himself empty after examining the bloodied corpses of men who were his friends and coworkers.

The men lay in postures that looked to McCutcheon like tintypes he'd seen of dead soldiers on Civil War battlegrounds. Surely this indeed had been a battlefield of sorts, though on a small scale. Maybe "battlefield" was too grandiose a word. This had been nothing but a slaughter pit.

What had been disturbing when seen from a distance was repellent and horrifying when seen close up. But it had also presented two mysteries.

Keith Dresden was not to be found among the dead. Nor was Jake Penn.

There also was no sign of anything that looked like a box of ransom money. Alone, this was not surprising in that the kidnappers would have no doubt taken the ransom with them. But had they taken away Dresden and Penn as well? Or had the two gotten away on their own?

Pale and shaken, Jeff Sampson approached Mc-

Cutcheon. He glanced down at the nearby corpse of Klugan and made a gagging noise. But he held himself together.

"I have to ask you something, Jim. About your partner, Penn."

"I knew you'd ask," McCutcheon cut in. "The answer is no: Penn would never become involved in any scheme to take money like that. No matter what."

"They say there might be more than half a million dollars," Sampson replied. "That would tempt even a good man."

"It would. But Jake would never give in to that temptation. I'd stake my life on it. And on him."

Sampson may or may not have been satisfied with that answer. Either way, he pursued it no further. "Then there's Dresden to think about."

"What do you think of him?" McCutcheon asked.

"Blain trusts him completely. My father seemed to think he's a good man. And he's been a good foreman. Not as good as Will Lincoln, I don't think, but good enough to please Abel Blain."

"But what's your own impression?"

Sampson shrugged. "He's a hard man to know. Keeps his thoughts to himself. But he's a hard worker, does whatever he does very well, and seems to have the respect of most everybody around him."

"But when it comes down to it, you don't really know him."

"Not well, not personally."

"Might he have taken the ransom for himself?"

"It's possible, I guess. But even then there's still your missing friend to consider. If Dresden took the ransom, what happened to Penn?"

"The honest truth is, Jeff, it's probable that Penn and Dresden are both dead, and we just haven't found their corpses yet."

"I guess we should look for more bodies."

"Yeah. And I have to say that I don't—" Mc-Cutcheon cut off, for he'd just seen Sampson's eyes make a quick dart to the rim of the canyon above them. Sampson had heard something up there, and Mc-Cutcheon had, too.

They were glad now they'd not brought the horses into the canyon.

"Got to hide," Sampson whispered.

They made for a nearby outcrop of rock and positioned themselves underneath it. They heard more noises from above. Horse hooves on stone. Faint voices carried to them by the natural acoustics of the canyon.

"Who do you think that is?" McCutcheon whispered.

Sampson shrugged. He looked scared.

McCutcheon was scared, too. He was glad he had his rifle.

Then again, the dead men in the canyon had also carried rifles.

"Which way are they moving?" McCutcheon asked.

"Back toward the mouth of the canyon, I think," Sampson replied.

The voices grew louder now. A man was talking angrily. McCutcheon could make out only the cussing, not any other content.

Sampson advanced a disturbing theory. "Maybe your partner and Dresden got away, and the ambushers chased them but didn't get them. Maybe they're coming back to look for the ransom money."

"We got to get away from here, Jeff."

"Yes . . . but how?"

There was no answer to that question.

Sampson swallowed hard, and his look hardened. A new resolve had swept through him. "We may die here," he said. "But I'll die taking as many as I can with me. They murdered my father."

McCutcheon was more interested in living than

dying. "Let's don't jump out shooting until we know who it is and what's going on."

"There's somebody already out there!" This was a sharp whisper from Sampson, who suddenly didn't seem so ready to die.

McCutcheon heard it, too. A man was moving along the canyon floor, heading toward them, and at the moment out of sight.

McCutcheon tried to form a plan. He could lunge out of the recess, confront the man, and perhaps shoot him down before the fellow could react. But this would expose him to the view of the others above.

All they could do, he decided, was hope the man wouldn't see them. Maybe he'd pass by.

It seemed unlikely. This recess was too shallow, and did not afford any real protection.

McCutcheon decided that Sampson was right. They were going to die here today.

He leveled his rifle, ready to shoot the sneaking man as soon as he appeared in front of the recess. Sampson raised his own rifle. This fellow would take a double blast, and probably never even know he was hit, much less by what.

A shadow moved on the ground as the man approached. A cloud that had been filtering the sunlight passed by and the sky brightened, intensifying the canyon's shadows.

McCutcheon lowered his rifle, reached over, and shoved Sampson's down as well, just as the approaching man was about to present himself.

McCutcheon had seen something familiar in that shadow. The posture of the man who cast it, his size, his general shape . . . he wasn't sure just what it had been, but he was not surprised when the face that appeared was that of Jake Penn.

"For Lord's sake, Cutch, you got to get out of

here!" Penn said. "They're coming back in, and there's not a moment to spare!"

"They'll see us, Jake!"

"Not at the moment. They're circling around toward the canyon mouth. If you run now, I can take you to a place where, just maybe, we'll have a chance of them not finding us. Dear Lord, boy, what made you come here now? I was just about to get out of this death trap when I saw you! Now none of us may make it!"

With those terrifying and chastening words, Mc-Cutcheon sprinted out of the recess. Penn, with one glance up to make sure all was still clear, began darting across the rocky canyon toward a jumble of rocks and talus on the far side.

McCutcheon glanced back. Jeff Sampson lingered at the opening of the recess.

"Don't hold back, Jeff! You can trust Jake Penn!"

Sampson hesitated a moment more, nodded, and ran out after them.

They ran hard, with only Penn knowing exactly where they were headed. But all knew that at any moment, the riders they had heard above would appear at the entrance of the canyon, and try to cut them all down. It provided a most compelling motivation to be fleet of foot.

Chapter Fifteen

Penn led them to another opening in the rocks, this one was much deeper, seemingly an entrance to a cave.

"Inside!" Penn commanded. "I don't think they know of this place . . . they didn't find it when they looked before. If we're lucky, they'll not find it now."

McCutcheon and Sampson asked no questions. They dove into the cool and welcome darkness. Penn followed.

"Back in deeper!" he said. "We want to be sure they can't look in and see us!"

The cave was low-roofed and none too big around, more a natural tunnel than a cavern. Once they were a few yards in, it curved, and all was pitch black beyond the turn.

"We're far enough . . . I hope," Penn said.

McCutcheon stopped. He was out of breath, more from tension than from exertion. He sat down on top of the stone behind him.

The stone, he noticed, was remarkably square and flat. He felt behind him. He couldn't tell exactly what it was, but it certainly was no stone. Its texture was much different.

"Who are they?" Sampson asked Penn, whose form was only the dimmest of outlines in the darkness. "The kidnappers?"

"I might first ask who *you* are, young man," Penn whispered back.

"Jake, this is Jeff Sampson," McCutcheon said. "He's one of Blain's cowboys, and me and him came to find you and the others once we realized what was going on."

"I'm not sure that I know what's going on myself," Penn replied, his tone softer now. "Pleased to meet you, Jeff. I rode with your father . . . I don't know whether he made it through the ambush or not."

"He was hurt," Sampson said. "He got out of the canyon, and Jim and me found him. He told us the kidnappers had attacked the riders as they came through the canyon. And then . . . he died."

"I'm sorry to hear that. He was a good man, and mighty friendly to me. I appreciated his company."

Penn's voice was extremely gentle; if not for the fact that they were enclosed in a narrow cavern, they probably would not have been able to hear him at all. He was taking great care not to be heard. "Fellows, I'm not trying to dispute the word of Jeff's late father, but I can tell you whoever committed that atrocity out there was definitely not the men who kidnapped Bethany Colby."

"How can you know?" McCutcheon asked.

"By exercising my common sense. Sampson would have come to the same realization if he'd had the time to think it through. Ask yourself: Why would kidnappers have to murder the ransom bearers to get the money, when they were having it delivered right to their doorstep already? There'd be no need for a massacre."

It was an obvious point, once made, and both McCutcheon and Jeff Sampson wondered why they hadn't come around to it on their own.

"So it was somebody trying to get the ransom for

themselves, before it could be delivered to the kidnappers," Sampson said.

"That's right," Penn replied.

"We ourselves ran into three men with that sort of notion," McCutcheon said. "Over near the mission. They thought we were the ransom riders. We dealt with them, though. I don't think they'll be a bother to us again."

"Do you have any idea who the ambushers in the canyon might have been?" Sampson asked.

"I have a strong suspicion," Penn said. "Fellows, Abel Blain was betrayed in the worst way. And this Judas is named Keith Dresden."

"Dresden!" Sampson exclaimed, a little too loudly. Penn shushed him instantly.

Sampson went on, his voice back to a whisper. "You're telling me that Keith Dresden led that massacre?"

"No, he didn't lead it. But I think he was behind it." Penn was staring at the spot where the cave tunnel turned. If anyone from outside entered, the meager bit of light would be obscured and give away the intruder's presence. So far the light remained unchanged—a good thing.

"Why do you think that?"

"Because I witnessed Dresden riding away, not even being shot at, while the others were murdered in cold blood. And he was leading the horse with the strongbox. He had the ransom, the very thing the ambushers had to be after, and yet he was being left alone. That tells me that the men doing the shooting knew they had no reason to stop him . . . that he was one of them."

"I can't believe that," Sampson said. "Abel Blain trusts Dresden as much as he trusts Will Lincoln. He's trusted him with his own niece's rescue! I can't believe Dresden would betray him."

"There's something else I saw, too," Penn said. "I looked up during the fight, and caught a clear look at one of the ambushers. I thought I was looking Dresden himself right in the eye. But it couldn't have been him, for exactly at that time he was down in the canyon. So I figured . . ."

"His brother," Sampson breathed, confronted with a conclusion he obviously did not want to face. "Raymond Dresden. 'Cotton,' they call him most of the time. He's an unpleasant man, I've heard. Harsh and prone to bossing folks around. They say that Keith Dresden, who can be pretty ornery himself most of the time, acts like a mouse when his brother's around."

"When I saw that face looking down at me, it seemed likely to me it was Keith Dresden's kin," Penn said. "I'd heard your own father mention that Dresden had a brother, Mr. Sampson, and this brother provided good horses for this little ransom expedition. He'd sworn he'd not revealed anything about the kidnapping to him . . . but what if he was lying? What if Keith told his brother the whole story, and the Dresden brothers saw themselves an opportunity to become richer by half a million dollars? It would be easy enough. They knew that the ransom would probably have to be carried into Mexico. They also knew that, in this part of the country, any journey into Mexico would lead right through this canyon. Easy enough for Keith Dresden, his brother, and whoever else he might have hired into the scheme, to gun them down like fish in a barrel. Then the money is theirs free and clear. The Dresden brothers pay off their help and ride away rich men."

"I just can't believe that," Sampson said. "There's got to be another explanation."

"Maybe there is. But your own father told me that Dresden apparently begged to carry the ransom alone at the beginning. Abel was smart enough not to allow that . . . but what does it say about Dresden? Your father took it as evidence that Dresden was brave and good-hearted, and apparently Abel did the same. But it might equally be that Dresden volunteered because he figured the easiest way to get the money would be just to ride off alone with it and never come back. That way, you don't have to go through the messy business of murdering your own friends and fellow ranch hands."

McCutcheon and Sampson thought it all through. "God have mercy," Sampson whispered. "But how could Dresden have seemed so trustworthy, if he's capable of doing something like that?"

"Some people have a skill that way," Penn replied. "That's why you see scoundrels rise to the places of highest power so often: They know how to imitate the characteristics of trustworthy men, when they're something entirely different."

Another question begged for an answer, and McCutcheon voiced it. "Jake, how did you survive the massacre?"

"By the sheer grace of God and the finding of this here cave," Penn replied. "I was shot at aplenty, but they never hit me. When I saw Dresden taking off with the horse and the strongbox, I grew suspicious real fast. I went after him, and shot his packhorse. He lost the box with the ransom. He tried to go after it, but I drove him back with gunfire. He fell, got wedged in some rocks, and was struggling to get out when I got hold of the strongbox . . ."

With a start, McCutcheon suddenly realized what the smooth, flat-sided object, which he'd initially mistaken for a stone, actually was. He reached down and touched the box, contemplating the fact that half a million dollars lay inside it.

"I'm not sure why I bothered to even get that strongbox. I expected at any moment to be shot down, but there was a lot of confusion. Your own father was putting up a devil of a fight, Mr. Sampson, and that drew attention away from me. I carried the box over to some rocks, and lo and behold, there was this cave. The entrance, you may have noticed, can't be seen unless you approach it just right, which I'd chanced to do . . . and which we'll hope our friends out in the canyon won't."

"So you've managed to save the ransom money!" Sampson declared.

"Yes, and maybe, Lord willing, we've still got a chance to save poor Bethany, too. If we can just keep these murderers from finding us here."

McCutcheon hadn't considered that just yet. If Dresden had gotten away with the money, Bethany Colby would be left in the hands of the true kidnappers, with no ransom left to buy her freedom.

Fully comprehending the sheer level of evil that would be required to make a man willing to steal money that was a young woman's only chance for life, McCutcheon loathed Keith Dresden and his brother, even though he'd never met either man.

But as he touched the box and thought about the wealth inside it, he realized how easy it would be, despite all moral protestations, to become bewitched by the prospect of easy, instant riches.

But at the price of a girl's safety, and the outright murder of several good and innocent men? No. McCutcheon could think of no amount of gain that could tempt him to go that far.

Sampson was evidently thinking similar thoughts. "I'll kill Dresden next time I see him," he said. "And his brother. Because of them, my father is dead. And a bunch of other good men, besides."

"You may get your chance at Dresden before you know it," Penn said, his voice softer than ever. "There's somebody coming in this tunnel."

Chapter Sixteen

Out in the Gajardo Canyon, up near its mouth, Cotton Dresden was dirty, tired, shaken, and full of fury at his younger brother.

For once in his life Keith Dresden had stumbled upon a truly fine opportunity, and had been wise enough to recognize it for what it was . . . and now it all was falling apart in the most absurd way possible. Cotton turned to his brother.

"Keith, I want you to tell me how it is that this could have happened. We had that box right there on the back of that horse, and all at once you lose it. And to a common darky, Keith!"

The scar on Keith Dresden's face was livid and seemed to be pulsing slightly, something that happened when he was angry or frightened or distraught. "He shot the packhorse, Cotton! The ransom box fell . . . I couldn't get to it because you and all our supposedly fine help wouldn't keep him off me! I couldn't even get close to that box. And when I fell—"

"Yeah, I saw that. Floundering like a fool, your leg stuck in a hole! It might even have been funny, some other time, *any* other time but not now! Meanwhile, that darky had vanished like a mist, and the strongbox, too. And we ain't found him yet, Keith! No trail out of the canyon, no sign he ran away or rode away . . . but yet he's not here, and neither is our money!"

"We'll find him," Keith Dresden said. "He's hid somewhere in this canyon, and we'll find him. He couldn't have got far with that strongbox."

"We'd better find him. We'd just better." Cotton turned and began to pace back and forth. "Hell, maybe we should have stuck with the original plan. You'd gained Blain's trust. Before long you'd have been able to get your hands into his money without such a . . . *mess*." Cotton waved at the dead bodies around them.

"Not this much money," Keith mumbled back. Normally a forceful man, he'd always been intimidated into hangdog muttering by his elder brother. "And we wouldn't have got it in untraceable cash, either." He paused, then added, "And it would have been my neck on the block as an embezzler if anything had gone wrong, not yours."

"Yeah? Well, my neck's on the block now, ain't it! I just led the murder of a whole team of ransom riders . . . all but one colored-boy magician who can make himself and half a million dollars disappear and not even leave a single track behind! And now that my neck's on the block, I got nothing to show for it. Not a penny. Hell, we did better than this back when we were robbing banks and trains!"

"We'll find him, Cotton. And we'll find the money. He can't have gone far."

Cotton Dresden snorted in disdain. "Get on with you, Keith. Keep an eye on our boys searching down there. I didn't trust them when we robbed banks with them, and I don't trust them now. If one of them finds that strongbox with no one to see him do it, he might try to run off with it."

"They don't know how much is in it, Cotton."

"No, but they're sure smart enough to know it must be plenty if we're willing to carry out such a massacre for it. Now get on. Maybe that nigra hid in one of the

caves around here. This blasted canyon's got plenty
of them.''

It was right then that a call came from down the
canyon. Dexter Jones was excitedly hollering something about tracks, and a hidden cave . . .

Inside the cave, Jake Penn and his two companions
glanced at one another nervously, even though they
were barely visible to each other in the darkness.
They'd heard Jones' shout, too; it had echoed back
through the cavern like a roar.

Jim McCutcheon was wishing hard right now that
he and Penn had never gone to the Blain ranch to
find work. Starvation would be better than being
slaughtered in a dark tunnel.

And death seemed inevitable. McCutcheon had just
crept back a few feet and found the concave rear wall
of the cavern. The cave went back no farther, not in
any size to accommodate a man, anyway. There was
no exit except the opening ahead.

They were trapped here in the dark, with armed
men about to come in after them.

"My friends, let's sell our lives dear, if we must,"
Penn whispered. "Take as many of them with you as
you can. Maybe, Lord willing, we'll actually be able
to gun our way out of here.''

Good old Penn. Always trying to keep hope alive.
McCutcheon appreciated it, but this time he couldn't
find Penn's optimism convincing. He could tell from
the way Penn had said it that he didn't really believe
it, either.

"You! Darky! You back in this hole?"
The voice came from the cave entrance. It sounded
as if the man was already crawling inside.
In the darkness, Penn held silent. McCutcheon

barely dared to breathe, and Jeff Sampson's heart pounded so hard it was audible.

Penn moved forward ever so slightly, changing position, readying himself to deliver a most violent surprise to the intruding man.

McCutcheon wondered if in fact there was some hope they could shoot their way out of this hole. He doubted it, trapped in here as they were. At best they might kill one or two who dared to actually enter the cavern, but that would simply make the men outside look for other means of killing those inside.

It was easy to imagine dreadful ways that they could die in this tomblike space. Fire, smoke, explosives . . . McCutcheon tried to shut off the dark thoughts. This was not how he wanted to die.

McCutcheon could feel Penn tensing as he readied to launch himself out to fire. He prepared himself for the deafening volume the shot would give out in this enclosed space.

The noise that actually came, though, was quite different than a gunshot. There was a strange, extended, almost moaning rumble that seemed to come from everywhere. A chorus of yells from outside the hole followed, then a scream of fright as the man entering the cave scrambled back to the opening.

Then a horrific crash, deafeningly loud, shook the entire mountain as if it was tumbling down.

The man trying to leave the cave screamed again, then was silent.

A cloud of choking dust filled the cave and grit crackled back through the tunnel as if shot from a cannon.

The entire cave was plunged into utter darkness. There was nothing but suffocating dust, a sense of enclosure, and a blackness deeper than any night.

Outside, the Dresden brothers and their companions picked themselves up from the ground and stared through billowing clouds of dust at a most remarkable sight.

A small rockslide, just one more of the many common in this canyon, had tumbled down the mountain and covered the entrance of the little cave that Dexter Jones had just entered, and from which he was desperately trying to remove himself when the rocks came down. They'd barely managed to scramble away in time to avoid being crushed.

As for Jones, there was no sign of him now. The stone, they were sure, had come down before he could get out of the cave.

"Dexter!" one of the hired guns hollered. "Dexter, are you alive?"

No answer came. Gravel and occasional fist-sized stones tumbling down the cliff in the aftermath of the full rockslide made crackling, rumbling noises, but no human voice could be heard among those sounds.

Chapter Seventeen

In the pitch-blackness inside the cave, Jeff Sampson sat up. "What happened?" he asked the darkness around him, coughing, his voice strained.

Penn was coughing, too. Because of his position, he'd received a more thorough blasting with dust and grit than the others. But he managed to speak.

"The cave . . . the entrance . . . it's covered. There's been a rockslide, and we're buried in here . . . trapped."

"Oh, no . . ." Sampson pulled out a matchbox and snapped off a match.

"No!" Penn said, recognizing from the sound what Sampson was doing. "Too much dust . . . wait until the air clears before you strike a match."

Sampson put his matches away. He hacked and choked, McCutcheon and Penn doing the same. The air was nearly impossible to breathe.

"Think they'll dig us out?" McCutcheon asked.

"I don't think they know for certain that we're in here," Penn said. "And if they did dig us out, what would they do to us after they did? Those men out there ain't exactly our friends."

McCutcheon coughed as he spoke. "Not our friends . . . but maybe they'd let us live . . . and there's no hope for us if we stay here. I've already checked the rest of the cave, and there's no other way out."

Penn was silent a few moments. "You're right," he

said. "Better a little hope than none. I reckon we'll have to take our chances with those devils out there."

"In that case, we need to yell to let them know we're in here," Sampson said.

"Wait a minute," Penn said, thinking further. "Just hold on before we do anything we may end up regretting. One of them was crawling back in here right before the rocks came down."

"Yes. But did he get out again before the rocks fell?"

"I don't know. Let me go see. We may not be alone in here, my friends."

Penn crawled forward through the enclosed, dust-choked atmosphere, traveling by feel alone. It was harder than he'd anticipated, and he bumped his head several times.

He reached the place where the new-fallen stones had piled back into the cavern entrance. Feeling all about, he tried to find a human form but detected none.

Either the man had gotten out, or he was buried under the rocks.

Penn listened, trying to hear noise from outside. He could hear nothing. The debris around the cave door was simply too thick for sound to come through.

Penn crawled back to the others, who still waited, coughing and scared, in the impenetrable darkness at the rear of the cave.

"He's not there," Penn said. "Must have got out, or got buried."

"If it's the latter, then they might dig for him," McCutcheon said.

"Maybe. It depends on how big the slide was. Too big a one, and they'll probably just leave him buried."

"But the ransom . . . they might dig out the slide hoping to find it hidden in here. You heard the man yell at the beginning, something about finding our tracks."

Penn couldn't know what to think. How hard the murderers outside might try to dig out this cave depended on too many unknowable factors—from the amount of debris, to their level of concern for the man who had tried to enter the cave, to their degree of suspicion that the ransom might be hidden inside.

Lacking enough information to decide what to do, the three trapped men simply remained where they were, breathing the dusty air and knowing that it would eventually run out, unless there was some natural ventilation they could not detect.

At least we'll die rich men, Penn told himself silently, thinking of the money-filled strongbox. It was an ironic thought, but not an amusing one.

Outside, the Dresden brothers were arguing, and this time, Keith Dresden was angry enough to assert himself a little more than he usually did around his intimidating brother.

"Not dig it out? What the hell do you mean, Cotton? We can't just walk away from this!"

"I didn't know you were so tenderhearted toward Dexter Jones," Cotton Dresden said in a mocking tone.

"I ain't worried about him! Even if I was, that stone has probably crushed him, anyway. It's the money I want! There were tracks at the front of that cave. That darky might have carried the money back inside. That would explain how he disappeared so fast in the midst of the fight, and why we could find no sign of him having left the canyon."

Keith looked over at the others, some of whom were already moving rocks, trying to reach the buried Jones. Others who hadn't known Jones well or who simply had disliked him, stood by, not caring to engage in such impossible labor unless directly ordered by the Dresden brothers. They were not men much prone to sympathize with others, even one of their own, who might be dying even now behind a blockade of stone.

"If he did leave the canyon, we'd be lucky to have found sign, anyway," Cotton replied. "And I believe he did leave. Some of them horses spooked by the gunfire ran on through and up out of the canyon, you know. He probably found one and rode off with the strongbox."

"Or he might be in the cave with the ransom, which is why we've got to dig it out."

"Think about this logically, Keith. If the ransom is in that cave, it's now buried. It won't go anywhere. But if the ransom is on the back of some horse with that darky in the saddle, then it's getting farther away from us by the minute. But in that case, there's a good chance we can pick up a trail and track the darky, and the money. But that option has a time limit. The trail won't last forever, and the longer we wait, the more chance the darky has to get away. On the other hand, if the money's in the cave, it's not going away. We can always come back later and dig it out, if we find no trail to follow."

Keith had to admit it made sense. It was unlikely anyone would disturb that ransom if it was cut off by several tons of stone. Cotton was right. Better to play on the possibility that the ransom had already left the canyon, and seek its trail before it grew hopelessly cold.

"All right," he said. "I'll go along with that."

Cotton Dresden nodded. "Knew you'd see the sense of it, brother." But then something seemed to come to mind. He put his hand to his chin, frowning, and thought hard for nearly a minute.

"What are you studying on, Cotton?" Keith asked.

"Just thinking this through. Tell me something: What kind of man does this colored fellow seem to be?"

"What do you mean?"

"Honest, or a cheat . . . that kind of thing. What's he like?"

"Well, Abel Blain surely thinks high of him. Apparently the pair of them saved each other's lives during the war. Blain talks like this Jake Penn is some kind of saint."

Cotton Dresden seemed intrigued to hear that. "And a saint might be too honorable to become a thief."

"What are you getting at?"

"That maybe, if Jake Penn has that ransom money, as surely he does, he may not try to keep it for himself like most would. He might still try to deliver it."

Keith Dresden hadn't considered that. Like most of his moral ilk, he'd naturally assumed that Penn would take the money for his own if the opportunity came.

"Does Penn know where the money is to be taken?" Cotton Dresden asked.

"He knows it's to go to Castillo. Beyond that, he doesn't know the exact details about where, or to who. Only I know that. I told no one else."

"So Penn would have to take the money to Castillo if he delivers the ransom . . . and once he got there, he'd have to figure out how to locate the kidnappers on his own. Which would take some time and effort."

Keith Dresden grinned, beginning to understand. "And time is opportunity for us to get our hands on the ransom again."

"That's right." Cotton was downright cheerful now. "We'll look for Penn's trail, but if we don't find it— as well we may not, considering the terrain and the fact that the nigra might be smart enough to cover his tracks—we'll go to Castillo, and wait for him."

Keith Dresden scratched his jaw, his brows knitting. "But Cotton, what if Penn gets there with the money, and somehow he manages to get it to the kidnappers before we get it away from him?"

"We can't afford to let that happen, can we!"

"No."

"Then we won't. You know where the kidnappers are to be met and the girl turned over, am I right?"

"That's right."

"All right. Then we will meet them, just as planned. But not on the same terms they intend."

"I'm not sure what you're getting at."

"There's plenty of time to talk about it on the trail. In the meantime, we need to ride. If we can overtake that darky, then it'll be easy to get our money. If not, we need to be sure to get to Castillo before he does."

Chapter Eighteen

Some of the others protested when they learned that no further attempt would be made to try to rescue Dexter Jones, but the protests were mostly token. It would take a long time to dig out the rockslide by hand, and there was always the danger of a new slide coming down on them while they did so.

Besides, if Jones was under that rock, or even trapped inside, he was as good as dead anyway.

The Dresden brothers and their surviving hired gunmen mounted and rode out of Gajardo Canyon in the direction of Castillo.

They simply left the dead behind on the floor of the canyon. They were glad to get away from them, as the vultures were already feasting.

"The air's cleared some . . . I think you can strike a match now, if you want, Jeff," Penn said.

They'd been sitting silently for maybe an hour. That was McCutcheon's guess, anyway. Remarkable how hard it was to follow the passage of time when there were almost no sensory reference points by which to measure it.

McCutcheon held his breath, listening to Jeff Sampson fumbling about, and waiting for the light of the match. He longed for light, yearned for it, even if only the momentary flare of a match.

Before long, he feared, it would be air for which he

yearned. Already it seemed that the breaths he took were not quite as satisfying and nourishing as they should be.

The sound of the striking match seemed abnormally loud. All three men flinched back from the little explosion of light, their eyes now accustomed to the full darkness.

By the match's light they looked around at their surroundings, hoping to see some previously unnoticed exit. There was none.

The match burned down to Sampson's fingertips. He dropped it reluctantly. Darkness returned.

"How many matches do you have?" Penn asked.

"I don't know . . . about a dozen. Maybe more."

"Come on," Penn said. "Let's move up toward the opening."

They did so, fumbling about in the dark.

"Another match?" Sampson asked.

"Yes."

This flare revealed their situation in all its ominous fullness. The match's light played over masses of tangled boulders of various shapes, most of them relatively small. None appeared too large to be rolled or pulled away, but the way they were stacked assured that the movement of one stone would probably only free another to fall into its place.

The second match went out.

"I'm going to tear some cloth from my shirt," Penn said. "We can light it. It'll give us a little longer light, and spare the matches."

"I've got a few matches myself," McCutcheon said. "And some quirly papers we could burn."

"Fire eats up air," Sampson pointed out.

"Yes, and so does exertion," Penn said. "But I intend to exert a little, and see if we can move these rocks and maybe find ourselves lucky. If some of those at the top can be made to tumble down, maybe they'll open up a way out."

This possibility brought hope. When Penn finished tearing away a cloth strip and gave the word, Sampson lit another match, and then fired the cloth. The light burned up brighter, smoke curling into the air.

Penn immediately pulled away a stone, then another. A third one rolled down of its own accord.

McCutcheon tore a cloth strip from his own shirt and lit it from the fading flame of the first one.

Sampson came to Penn's side and began pulling away stones, too. McCutcheon, meanwhile, pulled off his vest and began tearing it to pieces, using the fragments for fuel. The light was welcome, and essential to the work being done, but McCutcheon wondered how quickly the fire was using up the air in the cavern.

"Jake . . . look," Sampson said.

Penn had already seen. The last stone they'd moved had caused several others to shift. Revealed were the legs of a man.

They'd just found Jones.

The sight of a dead man sobered them all into inaction for a moment. But Penn shook himself out of it, and quickly studied the arrangement of the stones above the dead man.

"Quick," Penn said. "Grab a leg, and let's pull him straight back toward us."

"Grab a leg?"

"Don't get squeamish now, Mr. Sampson. I'm thinking that if we get him out from under there, that rock there might shift to the left, and the one above it, then the big one . . ."

He didn't need to say more. Sampson saw what he was getting at. As McCutcheon put another strip of cloth into the flame, they grabbed the dead man's calves, and pulled. It was no use. There was too much rock above him.

Quickly they went to work, tugging at the most obstinate boulder until their hands bled. Still, it wouldn't budge.

They all noticed, with none mentioning it, that it was growing harder to breathe.

McCutcheon joined them. With a great, combined effort, they finally moved the stone. It finally rolled to one side, and across the fire, snuffing it right away.

"I can get my matches and—"

"Never mind it, Mr. Sampson," Penn said. "We know where he is. Grab a leg and pull!"

They did. The body moved this time.

The results were dramatic. The heap of stones made a groaning sound, then shifted.

Penn, McCutcheon, and Sampson pulled back and away as the air filled with grit and dust again. Moving the corpse had caused a major shifting of the fallen stones.

Most wonderful of all, a beam of light pierced in through the rubble, and with it a marvelous, delicious gust of fresh air.

McCutcheon was so grateful, so joyous, that he feared he might weep. Penn and Sampson, meanwhile, laughed deliriously.

In moments, however, realizations came that tempered their happiness. The opening they had created was small, and high on the pile of rocks. It could easily close again if the rocks shifted in certain ways.

Furthermore, there was the fact that the gang of ambushers was still out there. Escape might lead them into a hail of lead.

They discussed these things quietly with one another. Then they grew quiet, and simply listened.

No sounds of human presence reached through the opening. They waited longer, and still heard nothing.

"I think maybe they've gone on," Penn said.

"I say let's dig," McCutcheon said. "We'll move

the stones carefully, to make sure we don't close the opening again."

It was terrifying, in a way, to begin the work. The thought of a wrong move causing new stones to tumble in and cut them off once more from the world outside was almost enough to overwhelm them. But they couldn't stay where they were. They labored carefully, painfully, for an hour, then two, then three . . . and the opening slowly grew bigger. A few stones from above tumbled in from time to time, but they were small, and easily dealt with.

At last, as the sun reached toward the west and the shadows outside grew long and oblique, they had opened for themselves a passage through the rockfall.

They flipped coins to see who would exit first. It was both a privilege and a danger to do so. The ambushers might be there still, waiting for them to emerge so they could be gunned down, and the ransom box claimed.

McCutcheon won, and worked his way out of the hole carefully. Stones shifted and snapped and cracked around him, but the opening did not cave in. He pulled himself out of it at the end, and rolled down the slanting, rocky heap of fresh-fallen stones.

He stood, bruised, dirty, and scratched, but alive, and looked up and down the darkening canyon.

No living human beings, other than himself, were present. The ambushers had gone.

Jeff Sampson emerged next, and tumbled down the same course McCutcheon had. When he stood, brushing himself off, he grinned at McCutcheon with his face nearly black with grit, and they shook hands.

Penn came last. McCutcheon and Sampson had removed their gun belts and left behind their long arms during their trips out the tunnel, just to make sure they fit. Penn shoved those items out ahead of him, and slid them down the slope to the younger men below.

Then he returned to the depths of the cave and brought out the strongbox. This he also slid down, where McCutcheon and Sampson received it, then stared at it, thinking about how much money was inside and about how exposed it, and they, were at this moment. Thank God the canyon was empty.

Penn made it out of the tunnel and down the slope. At Penn's suggestion, they all bowed their heads a moment and said a prayer of thanks for survival, thanks for open space and open air, and the beauty of being alive to see the sun setting.

They passed back through the canyon to its entrance, and up to where McCutcheon and Sampson had hidden the horses earlier. They fed the animals from the store of grain they carried in the saddlebags.

Another horse, saddled, roamed nearby. Penn recognized it as the horse that Doelin had ridden. Apparently it had turned and run back out of the canyon during the massacre. Penn claimed it for his own, to replace the fine horse that had been shot out from beneath him.

They rode back through the canyon again, passing through the massacre scene and the horrible, buzzard-pecked bodies. It seemed nearly sacrilegious to leave them lying untended, to be destroyed there in the open by nature's efficient but undignified methods, but there was nothing they could do for them. They did pause long enough to collect some of the dead men's weapons. The Dresdens obviously had possessed no interest in them and had simply left them with their dead owners. But Penn and company, outnumbered and outgunned as they were, felt a natural inclination to gather as many arms and as much ammunition as they could. It provided at least an illusion of greater safety.

It was growing dark now. They were hungry, and they made camp in a ravine well beyond the canyon and ate from the food Sampson had packed in his saddlebag. They made no fire because of the danger it created.

As long as the light held, they found themselves staring at the strongbox, thinking about the money in it, and how many men had already died because of it.

Chapter Nineteen

When they were through eating, they began to talk about what lay ahead.

"We've got ourselves an interesting situation, to put it mildly," Penn said. "It appears that to us has fallen the task of delivering this ransom money, but we've got a problem in that we don't know precisely where it has to go. Dresden said it was to be taken to Castillo, but who is to receive it there, and how we're to know them, and how we're to pass it to them . . . we know none of that."

"So what are we going to do?" McCutcheon asked.

"I was hoping you'd have an answer to that, because I don't," Penn replied.

"I think I do," said Sampson, quietly. "We just have to carry it on in, keep it safe, and just figure the rest out as we go."

"Keep it safe," McCutcheon repeated. "There's the real challenge. Half a million dollars in a box, and three men to watch over it."

"Not good odds," Penn conceded.

"We've got to do it anyway," Sampson said forcefully. "We can't let anything happen to Bethany. And I'd rather die than let the men who murdered my father go off unpunished. They'll never lay their hands on that strongbox again, not while I'm alive."

"There's the spirit," Penn said. "I feel the same way. But it won't be easy."

"Where do you think Dresden and his gunnies have gone?" McCutcheon asked.

"I figured they've headed for Castillo, hoping they can intercept us there," Penn replied. "They've obviously given up the notion that the money is still in the canyon. Either that or they figure it's still buried, along with us, in that cave where nobody can get to it. My guess is they're playing their options right now. Better to make sure the money wasn't carried off than to try to dig out a whole rockslide, only to find the money isn't there."

"They never really knew for sure we were in the cave," McCutcheon said. "Their man never crawled in far enough to actually find us."

"The truth is, we can't know right now where they are or what their scheme is," said Penn. "All I know is, I'm glad they've moved on. I'm tired of scrambling for my life."

"So what do we do? With the money, I mean."

"We'll just have to continue what we started and carry it to Castillo, like Mr. Sampson here said," Penn replied.

"Call me Jeff," Sampson said. "I agree with Jake. If we don't get that ransom into the right hands, Bethany is as good as dead."

"Have you considered that she might be dead already?" McCutcheon said.

Jeff Sampson gave him a sharp look. "Don't say that. I'll not consider it as even a possibility."

"I believe you must have a personal interest in the young lady, Jeff," Penn said.

"I just don't want her to be hurt. I couldn't bear that."

"Wait a minute," McCutcheon said. "Let's think this thing through. Say we take the money to Castillo without getting robbed or killed along the way. How will we know who to turn the money over to?"

"They've used pieces of her dress so far as their bona fides," Penn said. "I suppose they'll continue to do the same. Suffice it to say we won't turn over that strongbox to anyone who can't show proof they've got her."

McCutcheon said, "Penn, have you actually looked in that strongbox?"

"I ain't. I don't have the key."

"I wonder what half a million dollars looks like?"

"Best not to know. A wise man flees in the face of temptation."

"I'd not be tempted by it," Sampson said in an unintended but somewhat self-righteous tone. "That money means nothing to me except getting Bethany back safe again."

"What are the odds of us actually finishing this job?" McCutcheon asked. "We've got not only Dresden and his gang after it, but probably also every other piece of thieving trash in this vicinity."

"The odds are poor," Penn said. "But we're obliged to try our best." He stretched and winced. He was sore and battered. "I need rest," he said. "I'm too old for such adventures."

"You go ahead and sleep, Jake," McCutcheon said. "I'll take first watch, then wake up Jeff in a couple of hours."

When Penn was asleep, Sampson spoke quietly to McCutcheon.

"Penn seems to be a remarkable man."

"He is. The smartest, bravest, and best-hearted man I think I've ever known. He's a man who would die for you without a moment's hesitation, if he had to. He's loyal like nobody I've seen. He's been trying for years just to find his sister, who was separated from him many years ago. He can't even prove that she's alive, but he keeps going, keeps looking, because he's loyal to her."

"Why do you help him?"

McCutcheon looked away. "I've got nothing better to do. I've made some mistakes in my life, Jeff. I had a good opportunity, an inheritance from my parents, and I lost it. So I just ride with Penn, and try to help him out. And maybe learn a little from him about how to be a little bit wiser than I was before I met him."

"Do you think he'll ever find his sister?"

"Yes. If she's alive, I think he will. I guarantee you he'll try as long as he's living and able. It's just the way he is."

Sampson yawned, stretched, and said, "I'm tired, too. I'm going to lie down now. Don't forget to wake me up for my turn at watch."

"Sleep good, Jeff."

"Thank you."

"And by the way, Jeff . . . I'm truly sorry you lost your father."

"Yeah." Sampson shook his head. "It don't seem real, you know? I buried him with my own hands, and still I can't believe he's dead. I keep forgetting it happened. He was truly a good man."

"I don't doubt it."

"I don't intend his murder should go unavenged."

"Let's make sure it doesn't."

McCutcheon held his watch for an extra hour to give Sampson a chance for additional rest. Sampson, for his part, did the same, and never awakened Penn at all. As he assessed things, he saw how Penn's level-headed natural leadership had helped keep them alive during their ordeal in the cave. Penn's courage and quick action was the only reason the ransom money was not now in Dresden's possession, and now there still remained hope of buying back Bethany Colby's freedom.

The man deserved some sort of reward for that, if only an extra bit of sleep.

Penn was grateful. "Mighty fine of you to take into account an old man's frailty," he said.

"I only hope I'm as 'frail' as you when I get to your age," Sampson replied.

As they breakfasted on jerky and dried bread, Penn asked Sampson about his knowledge of the terrain, and the town of Castillo to which they were bound.

"I've been to Castillo only once, maybe two years ago," Sampson said. "I can get us there. It's a rough town. Not far from the border, you know, so it tends to attract a hard-edged kind of people, like border towns often do." He paused. "The thought of carrying that strongbox into that town is enough to send a chill down my back, to tell you the truth."

They used one of the extra horses as a packhorse, strapping the strongbox onto its back. They placed a couple of bedrolls on either side of the box and covered the entire thing with a saddle blanket, trying to disguise the strongbox's shape.

"Well, you can still tell what it is, I think," Mc-Cutcheon said. "But maybe not quite as easily."

"I know," Penn said. "It would be good if we could find a way to do this without being so obvious."

But ideas were lacking at the moment, so they had no choice but to proceed as they were. With Sampson guiding them, they rode. Penn, with his unusually sharp eyes, took the role of watcher, always scanning the landscape, looking for any evidence of others approaching or watching. A time or two he caught distant glimpses of riders, and once a flash of light from a low hillside, as if perhaps from reflected sunlight, but he couldn't be sure of it.

A couple of miles on, Penn halted his horse, studied something off in the distance to his right, then pointed in that direction. "Let's pay a visit over there."

"Why?" McCutcheon asked.

"I've got an idea."

Outside the rough, low little house they'd seen was a Mexican man in dirty, worn-out clothing. He'd seen neither razor nor hair scissors in many a week, and as they drew nearer, the expression on his face revealed itself as one of deep, weary sadness.

A rifle leaned up against a tree several yards from the man. With three mounted and armed strangers approaching him, it would not have been surprising to see him head for the weapon, but he merely stood there, slump-shouldered, with a hammer in one hand and nails in another, watching as they came closer.

"What are we doing here, Penn?" asked Mc-Cutcheon.

"Bettering our odds, if we can," Penn replied. "Just be patient. You'll see quickly enough what I've got in mind."

Chapter Twenty

A flatbed wagon beside the Mexican man was doubling as a worktable. On it was a new coffin, just nailed together.

On a bench up against the wall of the house was a wrapped body, obviously the intended future occupant of this box.

"Howdy," Penn said.

"Howdy," the Mexican replied.

"Death in the family?"

The Mexican looked puzzled. "Howdy," he repeated.

"Ah . . . *no habla* the American lingo, eh?" Penn looked around. "Sampson, dare I to hope you talk Mexican?"

Sampson dismounted and walked up to the Mexican, extending his hand. He spoke briefly to him in perfect Spanish. Penn arched a brow and glanced at McCutcheon, clearly impressed at this young man.

Sampson turned. "His name is Luis Martinez. His father has just died, and he's making a coffin to bury him."

"Tell him we're sorry to hear that."

Sampson spoke. Even in Spanish, his words carried a sincerity that Penn and McCutcheon could feel. Having just lost his own father, Sampson was situated to know how the Mexican man surely felt just now.

The Mexican replied at some length to Sampson.

Sampson translated again. "He says he's made this

coffin for his father, and once he has buried him, he plans to buy whiskey and drink until he dies. His wife left him when his father became sick, and took their children. He doesn't know where she is now, and doesn't want to live without her. He wants to join his father."

The Mexican spoke again, talking rapidly. Sampson visibly blanched as he turned to translate.

"He wants to know if we're the men carrying the ransom money to pay for the release of the kidnapped gringo girl," he said.

McCutcheon declared, "Lord! Just how far has this story spread?"

"Half a million dollars speaks with a loud voice," Penn said. He addressed Sampson. "Tell him not to drink himself to death. Tell him life is good and we want to strike a bargain with him."

McCutcheon wondered what Penn had in mind. One thing about Penn: He was always one step ahead, seeing around the next corner before anybody else got there.

Sampson spoke. The Mexican brightened considerably. Apparently his grief and weariness with the world had not sufficiently set in to make the prospect of making a little money unattractive.

Smiling, Martinez gestured enthusiastically for Penn and McCutcheon to dismount and enter his house.

McCutcheon took a quick look around the surrounding landscape before they did, afraid they were being watched. If they were, the watchers were well hidden. He hoped none were there at all.

Inside the house, they ate at their host's invitation. It bothered McCutcheon to do it, not so much because the tortillas were old and stale and the spicy sauce served on them not really fit to be edible, but because this was clearly the last food that Martinez possessed. It didn't seem right to eat the last a man had.

Penn and Sampson, in the meantime, conversed with Martinez again, and at last Penn's scheme became clear.

McCutcheon couldn't help but feel amused by the expression on Sampson's face as he finally understood what was going on. McCutcheon had been around Penn long enough to become accustomed to the man's innovative, even quirky, ideas. Sampson hadn't, and even as he translated Penn's proposal to Martinez, looked thoroughly astonished at what he was saying.

Martinez accepted Penn's odd proposal very quickly, once he understood that money was involved. But he added one proviso.

"He says he'll take our deal, but only if he can come with us," Sampson translated to Penn. "Frankly, I don't understand that. Why would he want to be part of a group of men who will be lucky to live to see next week?"

"Good question. Why don't you put it to him?" Penn replied.

Sampson did, then conveyed Martinez' answer to Penn. "He says there are three reasons he wants to come with us. First, he has nothing left here that he wishes to stay for. Second, he feels sorry for the kidnapped girl. Third, he says he figures that Abel Blain is a very rich gringo who would be very grateful to any humble Mexican farmer who helped rescue his girl."

"Ah, the old money incentive. The motive behind most of life's actions. Well, tell him I admire his honesty, but that we can't use him. The deal I offered for the coffin stands, but not with his proviso. He can't come along with us."

Martinez seemed disappointed but, as Penn anticipated, he still accepted the deal. As soon as the money was in his hand, his disappointment seemed over.

Following Penn's instructions, Martinez went back outside and began sawing the coffin lid in half. When they were done eating, his three guests followed him outside and watched him work.

As Martinez labored, Sampson wandered over and stared at the sheet-enwrapped corpse of Martinez' father, lying stiffly on its bench. A lazy dog came up to give the corpse a good sniffing over, and Sampson shooed it away.

McCutcheon joined Sampson in looking at the dead man. "It's a shame the poor fellow will have to be buried without a coffin," he said.

"Let me see if I understand exactly what we're about to do," Sampson said to McCutcheon. "Jake Penn has just bought that wagon and coffin, and he intends to ride inside the coffin, armed."

"Yes," McCutcheon said, "with the strongbox hidden at his feet."

Sampson nodded. "And that's why he's having Martinez saw that lid in half . . . so the part covering Penn's legs, and the strongbox, can be nailed down."

"Right," McCutcheon said. "And the upper part will just be laid into place, or tacked on so loose that Penn can push the lid open if need be. There'll be some air holes drilled in the sides, naturally."

"Why do you think Martinez was so quick to accept that bargain? He'd made this coffin for his father, and now his father's going to be buried in nothing but a sheet."

"A hundred easy dollars is why he did it," McCutcheon said. "He's probably never had that much money at one time in his life. And all he's got to give up is his father's coffin and a wagon that's so broken down that it's hardly worth buying for any amount, much less what we're giving him."

The money Penn had paid Martinez was leaving a vacant feeling in McCutcheon's pocket. Penn had taken the payment out of the money he'd given McCutcheon on the porch of the Blain ranch. But

McCutcheon didn't begrudge it. Penn's plan appeared
to him to have some real merit. Anything that might
help keep them alive long enough to get this ransom
delivered was worth the loss of a bit of money.

"Do you really think we're going to be safer this
way?" Sampson asked.

"Of course we are. Think about it. Here we are,
three men, one of them black. We're easy to identify.
Furthermore, we're hauling a strongbox on the back
of a horse. But now we won't look the same. Penn
will ride in the coffin with the money, and you and
me will put on ponchos and big Mex hats from our
new friend here. All at once, from a distance, we look
like two Mexicans hauling one of our dear departed
to the church at Castillo for burying."

Sampson said, "I can't persuade myself it'll work.
It seems loco."

"Well, I'd rather have Dresden see two Mexicans
and a coffin than two white men and a black one with
a strongbox. Wouldn't you?"

Martinez finished his sawing. Penn walked over and
examined the job.

"Very good," he said. "Jeff, tell him to nail down
the bottom half."

Martinez apparently understood at least a little English, because he hopped to this task enthusiastically,
without waiting for Sampson to translate the order.

Martinez quickly finished his hammering and beamed
at his companions. For a grieving man who'd been talking suicide by alcohol only a little while earlier, he'd
made a dramatic turnabout in attitude. Amazing what
a hundred dollars could buy, McCutcheon thought.

"I think we're obliged to help him bury his father,"
McCutcheon said.

"Agreed," replied Penn. "Tell him we'll give him a
hand digging the grave, Jeff."

There was no need for it, though. Martinez, knowing his father's impending death, had been digging the grave for days.

He wept silently while they lowered the wrapped body into the hole. Penn felt guilty at this moment for having taken away the coffin Martinez had intended for his father, though he was sure that, at this point, Martinez wouldn't go back on the transaction even if offered the chance.

Chapter Twenty-one

Jake Penn stared at the dark expanse of wood above him and pondered the strangeness of his situation. Though all men at some point ride in a coffin, most never have the opportunity to study the underside of its lid while they do so.

"How you faring in there, Penn?" It was McCutcheon's voice, from outside. McCutcheon was riding beside the wagon that bore the coffin.

"I feel like a dead man," Penn replied.

"Well, you don't *sound* dead."

"Good. Any sign of trouble out there?"

McCutcheon paused. "None so far."

"You don't sound certain."

"Jeff says he thinks he might have seen somebody following us."

"Martinez?"

"Maybe. He's not sure."

"Blast it! I told that Mexican we didn't want him coming with us!"

"It may not be him. It might be somebody else tracking the ransom money."

"Where's Jeff?"

"Up ahead, leading the wagon horse."

Penn wouldn't try to talk directly to Sampson, then. He'd have to holler to be heard, which would do nothing to enhance the illusion that the occupant of this coffin was deceased.

Penn moved his feet and felt his boot toes bump up against the strongbox. *I'm in a coffin with a pistol in each hand and a fortune at my feet,* he thought. *I'd be willing to bet this ain't going to happen twice in my life.*

Penn wondered if Martinez had laid his father in this coffin at any point to test the fit. He hoped not. Penn wasn't squeamish, but he'd rather not occupy a space where a corpse had lain.

He wished he'd made the airholes bigger. The atmosphere in this box was growing very stuffy.

Penn gently thumped the side of the coffin, just loud enough for McCutcheon to hear it.

"Go ahead and speak," McCutcheon said. "We still seem to be alone."

"How long until we reach Castillo?" Penn said.

McCutcheon conveyed the question up to Sampson, then relayed back the answer: "Jeff says we should get there sometime after dark."

That suited Penn in one way. They'd be less noticeable traveling by night. But it also meant he had a lot of time in this box still ahead of him.

Maybe he should try to sleep. But it was hard to relax on a cold slab of wood, with the coffin's sides squeezing his shoulders and his nose nearly scraping the underside of the lid.

Claustrophobia was beginning to set in. He closed his eyes and tried to imagine he was somewhere else.

"Whoa," Sampson said up ahead, softly. "Whoa, there."

The wagon lurched to a halt. McCutcheon rode up beside Sampson.

"What did you see?"

"Two riders," Sampson replied, nodding toward the east. "Heading in our direction."

"I don't see them."

"They've moved behind that grove of trees. Unless they stop there, they ought to be coming out soon."

"Armed?"

"Appeared so."

There was a gentle thump from inside the coffin. McCutcheon turned his horse and went back a few feet, and then whispered, "Penn, best be still and quiet. Riders nearby, Jeff says. Two of them."

He rode back up to join Sampson. "Let's keep moving."

They advanced again. McCutcheon wondered if Sampson had actually seen riders, or just imagined them. It seemed to him that Sampson was growing moody, quiet, distracted perhaps. Probably it was grief over his slain father. Probably he was only just now beginning to truly grasp the fact that Walt Sampson had been murdered. Maybe hauling around a coffin was driving that point home to the young man.

McCutcheon studied Sampson's form, then his own. Both of them wore ponchos they'd obtained from Martinez. Sampson had traded his former cattleman's wide-brimmed hat for a big Mexican sombrero, formerly property of Martinez' late father.

From a distance, they should have looked like nothing more than two Mexicans hauling a deceased friend or relative off for burial, not like men carrying ransom.

They rode on. McCutcheon began to relax. He'd nearly concluded that Sampson had in fact imagined the two riders, when he himself caught a glimpse of them.

Not two riders, though. Three. Or was it? They remained on the far side of the grove of brush and trees, keeping pace with the rolling coffin wagon, not exactly hiding, but not fully showing themselves either.

When they rode into a clearer spot, McCutcheon could finally see that there was just two of them.

The strangers turned their horses toward the wagon and rode into clear view.

"Here they come," Sampson muttered.

McCutcheon nodded. He didn't like this at all. And he didn't like the fact that, in moments, these riders would be close enough to see that the two "Mexican" coffin-haulers were in fact gringos.

"Be ready in there, Penn," McCutcheon said as loudly as he dared. "They're coming our way."

The riders slowed as they drew near. They wore faint smiles, carried themselves in a slumped and casual manner seemingly designed to make them seem relaxed and nonthreatening. It didn't work. Both carried weapons, one holding a shotgun, the other a Henry rifle.

One of the two was red-haired and clean-shaven, with heavily freckled skin and a left eye that wouldn't open all the way. The other man was swarthy, with a beard that was all tangles. He was bald above the ears, and wore a bowler hat and a mean look that his forced grin couldn't hide.

"Howdy, friends," said the red-haired man.

"Hello," McCutcheon replied.

"Thunk you was Mexicans when we seen you from a distance."

No reply seemed merited.

"Had a death in the family, have you?" the stranger asked, nodding toward the coffin.

"Death of a friend."

"Ah. Sorry to hear that."

"Your sympathy is appreciated."

"How'd your friend die?"

"Smallpox," McCutcheon replied, hoping this might drive these intruders away.

In fact, their smiles instantly faded. "Smallpox!"

"Worse case I ever seen. Sure hope I ain't caught it myself, though I fear I have."

The pair backed their horses away a little. Their

fulsomely friendly manner was now gone, and McCutcheon wondered if he'd said just the right thing to end
this little meeting, or make it explosive.

"I need to tell you something," the red-haired man
said. "You fellows might be in danger, riding along
like this."

"How so?"

"There's been a kidnapping up in Texas. Daughter
of a rich rancher. They say the ransom riders are coming through . . . them that survived one hellacious
massacre in the Gajardo Canyon."

"What does that have to do with us?" McCutcheon asked.

"There's always the chance somebody's going to
think that maybe you're the ransom riders."

"They might think the same about you."

"Yes. And we're being careful for that very reason.
We just wanted to advise you to do the same."

"Mighty righteous of you," McCutcheon said. "We'll
be heading on now. And we will be careful."

The red-haired man said, "Wait a minute. Are you
sure that your friend there died of smallpox?"

"I am."

"Because, you know, I'm kind of worried now that
maybe now I might catch it. And I don't like to worry.
So I'd like to see your dead friend myself, just to
know for sure what the facts is. If he died of smallpox,
it'd show."

"The coffin's nailed shut."

"How long's he been dead?"

To McCutcheon's displeasure, Sampson picked that
moment to make his first contribution to this conversation, and said precisely the wrong thing. "Three
days," he said.

"Three days?" The red-haired man looked deeply
skeptical. "Mighty odd we don't smell him, then.
Mighty odd indeed."

"We'll move on now," McCutcheon said.

The red-haired man leveled his shotgun, aiming it at McCutcheon's middle. "You'll go nowhere. I want to see your dead friend. For you know, it may be there's not a dead man at all in there. Maybe that's why we don't smell him. There's other things that can be carried in a wood box."

"Put that shotgun away," McCutcheon said loudly, to make sure that Penn knew the situation.

"Pull your hands out from under them ponchos, both of you," the man ordered. To Sampson he said, "You, skinny—get down off that horse and open that coffin up."

But this would not be necessary. The coffin top burst upward so suddenly that even McCutcheon and Sampson were startled.

The man with the shotgun turned his weapon toward Jake Penn, who sat upright like a reanimated corpse, both hands wrapped around pistol butts.

Penn and the man fired simultaneously, the man letting go with both barrels, and Penn blasting away with both pistols.

The entire top end of the coffin, just behind the upright Penn, exploded into splinters. Had Penn still been reclining, he would have been blown apart along with it.

Penn's shots hit flesh. The red-haired man was pounded backward, right over the rear of his horse, and hit the ground hard. He grunted, groaned, then tried to rise. The shotgun was somehow still in his hand, and he moved to raise it.

Penn ignored him, knowing the weapon was empty. His attention was now on the bearded one, who had brought his Henry rifle up and around—but too slowly. Again Penn blasted both barrels of his pistols. The man spasmed, firing off his rifle without aiming it, then pitched from the saddle sideways and slammed the ground. He did not move after that.

The man with the shotgun clicked the hammers of his weapon uselessly, staring with wide eyes at Jake Penn.

"You got to reload it before it'll work," Penn told him.

The man slumped to the ground and died, still holding the shotgun.

"I guess that's over, then," Penn said.

"I'm shot," Jeff Sampson said, his voice thin.

Penn snapped his head around and looked at Sampson, who gripped his left arm. Blood poured through his fingers.

That last random shot fired off from the Henry rifle had struck a target after all.

Before anyone could react to Sampson's words, a distant, cracking sound reached them, and a slug sang less than an inch to the right of Jake Penn's ear, tearing right through McCutcheon's poncho.

McCutcheon let out a yelp, and fell from his horse.

Penn came out of the ruined coffin and was at McCutcheon's side in two moments.

Sampson adopted a partial crouch and pivoted right and left, desperately looking for the source of the gunshot.

"Cutch! Are you shot?"

McCutcheon sat up, examining the hole in the poncho he wore. "No . . . went through the cloth, not me. I think I felt it graze just past me—"

The next shot suddenly slapped the ground a foot from Penn.

"There!" Sampson shouted. "I saw where that one came from!" He raised his rifle with his good arm and fired in return. But aiming was hopeless for him and the slug burrowed into the ground far short of its target.

Penn and McCutcheon separated, diving in different directions and rolling. Unlike Sampson, they'd not seen the burst of the shot and did not know where to shoot.

"There!" Penn said. "There he is . . . running through those trees."

"Wait a minute . . ." McCutcheon said. "Was that—"

"Martinez," Sampson said. "That's him."

"You're telling me that Martinez is shooting at us?"

"Seems that way," Sampson replied. Now that they were in new danger, his voice suddenly was stronger, and he was ignoring his bleeding arm wound.

But another shot blasted, another slug zipped past. Clearly it had come from a place ahead of where Martinez would have been.

"It ain't Martinez shooting at us!" Penn said. "In fact, I think he's—"

Three fast shots resounded in the grove, the sound slightly muffled by the foliage, which also blocked out the muzzle flashes.

A silence settled across the land.

Then Martinez appeared at the front edge of the grove, a rifle in each hand. He raised them high and shook them triumphantly.

Even from this distance, McCutcheon could see the grin on Martinez' face . . . then he noticed a scope on one of the rifles.

Suddenly something clicked in McCutcheon's mind. He realized he'd seen the two men Penn had shot down once before: It was they who had entered that gunshop in Black Hill, and come out with weapons, one of them a scoped rifle.

Martinez came toward them on a trot.

Several minutes later, Penn, McCutcheon, Sampson, and Martinez stood in the grove from which the shots had come, and stared down at a third dead gringo, shot to death by Martinez.

"It looks like we do indeed owe Mr. Martinez our lives," Penn said. "This sniper would certainly have killed one or all of us if Martinez hadn't gotten him first. That's a powerful scope on his rifle. Jeff, please express our thanks to our friend here. Though he disobeyed our instructions not to follow us, I can't be angry at him about it, considering the outcome."

Sampson, still gripping his injured arm, translated. Martinez nodded humbly and smiled.

McCutcheon spoke in a low tone. "Penn . . . what now?"

"I don't know," Penn replied. "We do have to wonder what Martinez' motive was in coming after us."

"He could have it in mind to get the ransom for himself," McCutcheon said softly.

Penn nodded. "Yes. And so these three who are now dead would have been, in his mind, competition. His helping us deal with them might have been selfishly motivated. Or, it could be that he's just a good-hearted man who's doing this solely for our own good."

McCutcheon said, "Again I ask: What do we do with him now? We can't know he's trustworthy."

Sampson had picked up on their conversation. "I believe we can trust him," he said. "If Martinez wanted to hurt us, why didn't he just take that scoped rifle and gun us down himself? Or just let the original sniper do it, and *then* kill him and take the money?"

Martinez stood off to the side, watching and listening to a conversation he couldn't understand.

Sampson went on. "He took quite a risk, approaching this sniper in this grove. He could have just held still, committed a quick murder after we were all dead, and there'd have been no one here to stop him from taking every cent of that ransom for himself."

"Maybe you should just ask him why he followed us when he was told not to, Jeff," McCutcheon suggested.

Sampson turned and faced Martinez. He spoke Spanish to him.

Martinez answered softly. Sampson turned and translated. "He says he followed us for all the reasons he gave before, and because he has nothing better to do, with his father dead. He feared we would need more protection than we were able to give ourselves."

"Do you believe him?" McCutcheon asked Penn.

Penn thought about it. "I do. I think Jeff's instincts are right. And the truth is, there might be some good use for him once we reach Castillo. Dresden doesn't know him. But he does know me and Jeff. He may even know you, Jim, if he caught a glimpse of you when we arrived at the Blain ranch. I think we need Martinez along after all."

McCutcheon thought it over. "Very well. I just hope we're not going to regret it later on."

That issue settled, Penn turned his attention to Sampson's injury. The slug had torn the flesh of his arm badly, but had passed clear through. Still, the wound needed attention from a doctor.

"You may have to turn back, Jeff," Penn said. "I doubt you'll find decent medical care in Castillo."

"I'll not turn back," Sampson replied. "Bind it up. I'll make do until I can find a doctor. There'll be somebody in Castillo who can take care of it, I feel sure."

Chapter Twenty-two

They reached Castillo after nightfall, and even by dark, Penn didn't think he'd ever seen an uglier town.

Castillo was a village that was for the most part the color of the landscape around it. Built mostly of adobe, its buildings were predominately low, rectangular, and ugly. The town had a wide central street with a well in the middle of it, but other than that seemed haphazardly designed, if it was even designed at all.

A church at the far edge of the town featured an imposing tower that looked down on the unholy squalor below. And unholy it was, Sampson had told them. Castillo was a dangerous, wild town, lawless in the most literal sense. There was no town government beyond a thoroughly corrupt board of overseers under the hire of a gaggle of wealthy and criminal men whose ornate houses stood somewhere in the dark wilderness well beyond the town. There was no body of town laws and no officials of any kind to provide order or protection.

"That's probably why the kidnappers chose this town as the place to receive the ransom," Penn had said after Sampson described Castillo's famed lawlessness. "There's no chance of law intervening when there *is* no law."

They were in shadows now, hiding up against an empty building at the eastern end of town. They gazed across a street so wide it was more like a central plaza than a street at all, and listened to the noises of Castillo after dark.

Music spilled out from more than one of the several lighted cantinas along the street. An out-of-tune guitar inflicted torture upon an old Mexican folk tune in one saloon, while a rattly piano competed with it from another.

There were voices, shouts, arguments, laughter, all mixing together, riding the wind that blew through the town and kicked up dust. A small whirlwind spun a funnel of grit down the midst of the street, engulfing the well, then blowing past. Two drunks staggered by, and on the far side of the street, two angry men waved knives at each other, trading curses and threats.

As Penn examined the scene, he realized that they were not the only men hidden in darkness. In many a shadowed alley he could make out barely visible forms, and the occasional red flare of a cigarillo as some unseen smoker drew upon it.

Penn had seen many such towns in his time, spread across the United States, Canada, and Mexico. Different as they were in name, geography, and appearance, they all shared a similar, unidentifiable quality that Penn had grown able to recognize at once, like a familiar and unpleasant stench. Castillo had it, and it made hackles rise on the back of his neck.

He eyed the dark church tower and wondered if the church's presence here had any impact at all upon the behavior of the people who inhabited, or visited, Castillo. He doubted it.

"I generally try to avoid towns like this," he muttered to McCutcheon. "A man finds nothing but trouble in such a place."

"Especially when he's carrying half a million dollars in a strongbox," McCutcheon replied.

"What now?" asked Sampson.

Penn pointed toward one of the few structures in the town, other than the church tower, that stood higher than a single story.

"Is that a hotel?"

Sampson squinted, reading the sign above the door. "Yes, it is."

"I think we ought to take up lodging there. Top floor, if we can."

"Why the top floor?"

"Because it's high enough that it would be hard to reach it from the outside. And high enough to provide us a view of the street and alley below, if we get the right room."

"So we'll take the strongbox right into the hotel with us?"

"Better that than guarding it down here."

"Maybe they have a safe. Or maybe there's a local bank with a vault."

"Not interested," Penn said. "This money isn't going out of our sight, or under any lock and key that anyone besides us can control."

Another drunk staggered past, not noticing the four men watching from the shadows. This one was a gringo. A moment later, another gringo passed, his arm around a gaudily dressed cantina girl. Penn was glad to see the combination of Americans and Mexicans here. They would not stand out as readily as they would in a town without a mix of races and cultures.

So far, though, he'd spotted no other black men. He would stand out even if his companions didn't. And by now it was possibly widely known that a black man was among those who bore the ransom for the kidnapped American girl.

Penn said a quick silent prayer: *Lord, do not let me be a danger to those who ride with me.*

"How do you want to go about checking in to the hotel?" McCutcheon asked.

"We'll circle around the outside of town and come in through that alley over there beside the hotel," Penn said. "Then we'll let Martinez go in and rent rooms for us. If we can get them, I want the top-floor rooms on the front and corner of the building."

"Penn," McCutcheon asked, "now that we're here . . . what are we going to do with the ransom? We've brought it to Castillo, but how do we know who to deliver it to? Or exactly where?"

"One thing at a time, Jim," Penn said. "We're pretty much going to have to figure this out as we go."

Luckily, the rooms Penn wanted were available. Martinez quickly rented them.

Penn paid a stable boy to tend to the horses, then, with care and a carefully placed saddle blanket, the group of them managed to slip the strongbox into the hotel without drawing much attention.

They locked themselves into one of the two connected rooms, sat the strongbox onto the floor in the midst of it, and for a few moments stared at it as a group.

"What now?" McCutcheon asked. The question was directed at Penn. No one had made Penn leader of the group in any formal fashion, yet no one questioned that he was in charge. Penn was a natural leader. He fell into the role without effort, and others instinctively stepped aside to let him do it.

"We're in something of a blind alley," Penn said. "We've gotten the money to the right town, but we don't know exactly who to take it to, or where, or how to recover Bethany Colby."

"Meanwhile, we've got a wounded man needing medical help," McCutcheon said, glancing at Sampson.

Sampson made as if to argue that he in fact needed no care, but the effort faltered away. He was hurting, in danger of infection, and couldn't deny it. His face had a thin, drawn look.

Penn thought things over a few moments. "We're going to have to divide up. Somebody needs to find a doctor, or the nearest thing to one we can locate . . . maybe Martinez can do that. He can speak the language, ask the right questions, and nobody knows he's one of us."

Sampson conveyed the request to Martinez, who nodded quickly, seeming quite eager to help.

McCutcheon looked at Martinez distrustfully. Penn noticed it, and noted to himself that he didn't share McCutcheon's obvious doubts. His instincts about Luis Martinez were positive. It was proving to be a good thing that he'd followed and joined them.

"Jeff, you and Jim can stay here and guard the strongbox," Penn said. "Could you shoot if you had to, Jeff?"

"Yes . . . but do you think somebody would actually try to take it from us right here in the hotel?" he asked.

"There's been plenty of people ready to try to take it in every other kind of circumstance. Why not here?"

"Do you think that Dresden and his brother know we're in this hotel?"

"I have no idea. It's possible Dresden's not even in Castillo."

"Possible, but not likely," McCutcheon said. "They'd not give up that fast on trying to get the money. Not after all the killing they've done."

Penn nodded in agreement.

"Are you going to stay here and help us guard this strongbox?" Sampson asked Penn.

"No. I'll be around town. Trying to find some kind of clue about where we are to deliver that money. I'm sorry I have to leave you here alone to do it. If anyone can see a better way, though, I'm willing to listen."

No one had any suggestions.

McCutcheon asked, "How do you propose to learn what you need to learn out there, Penn? You can't just go around saying, 'Pardon me, folks, but I've got half a million dollars of ransom to deliver and need to know where to take it.' "

"I don't know how I'll go about it," Penn admitted. "All I know is, I got to try. I'll just hope for providence and good instincts to show me the right way to go about it. And the safe way."

"I doubt there is a safe way," Sampson muttered.

"I'm afraid you're probably right, Jeff. But let's all keep in mind we're doing this for Bethany Colby, who is by no means safe, either. It's a lot worse for her than it is for us."

Chapter Twenty-three

Martinez walked slowly through Castillo, trying to decide how best to proceed with his assigned mission.

He wasn't comfortable here. Though he'd never been one to shun cantinas and alcohol, and had seen his share of fights and trouble, Martinez generally avoided towns as rough as Castillo. He'd been here only once before. He'd almost gotten himself killed that time, and had sworn not to return.

Yet here he was . . . and he wasn't sure why. He'd not really had a reason to follow these coffin-buying, ransom-carrying strangers, and join their effort. But with his father dead, there'd been nothing else for him. And the three strangers had a purpose, at least, a goal, an adventure before them, and a good reason to undertake it.

He'd felt compelled to follow. And compelled to intervene when they'd been in danger of being murdered by that sniper in the grove.

It was hard for him to believe he'd actually killed a man. Yet he didn't really regret it. he couldn't allow men on so worthy a mission as the rescue of a kidnapped young woman to be killed by some cursed sniper.

He glanced into a brightly lighted cantina, where a buxom woman in a tight-fitting dress carried a tray laden with crockery jugs overflowing with Mexican beer. She caught him looking through the open door, smiled, and winked at him. He smiled back and was about to enter the cantina, but stopped, stricken by conscience. He had a job to do.

With some regret, he turned away and walked farther up the street, looking about for some indication of where a *médico* might be found. It was quite possible there was no proper one, but surely the rough, brawling populace of Castillo had to have somewhere to go to get their stab wounds and bullet punctures tended.

He noticed a *tienda* nearby that had not yet closed for the evening. A simple general merchandise store, it appeared. He headed for it.

The merchant inside was in the process of closing down, and asked him to return the next day, if he could.

"I need nothing but information," Martinez said in Spanish. "Is there a doctor in this town?"

"Are you sick?"

"No. But there is a friend of mine who is hurt. He was stabbed."

"Ah, yes. Well, there is no doctor. Only a priest who sometimes helps people who are hurt."

"A priest . . . he is in the church?"

"Yes. He's a lonely man, I suppose. Not many people in Castillo follow the ways of God."

"What is his name?"

"Father Mateo. He is a good man."

"I'll go to him."

"Good, but remember: He is a priest, not a doctor. He may not be able to help your friend."

It was unnecessary to ask directions to Father Mateo's church. Its spire was the most noticeable feature of the Castillo skyline.

Martinez left the store and headed toward the church. The chapel, with its high, adjacent tower, was surrounded by a high wall. He did not at once see a gateway through it.

He headed toward the wall, which was heavily shadowed by trees growing on both sides of it.

Martinez paused before entering the shadows.

He didn't think he was alone here.

He turned to his right and tracked along the side of the wall, hoping to reach a door soon. He prayed that when he did, he would find that door unlocked.

In the shadows behind him, something moved. He was being followed . . . was it someone who had watched him leave the hotel, and trailed him here?

He began to wish he'd not involved himself with the ransom riders after all.

He hurried on.

Penn was gone, and McCutcheon wished he wasn't.

Even the presence of levelheaded Penn, though, probably would not do all that much to overcome the jitters McCutcheon felt. Even if he had a dozen other capable men in this room, helping guard that blasted strongbox full of cash, he'd probably still feel edgy. It was absurd, really: a half-million dollars in cash, locked in a common strongbox in a hotel room in a town full of thieves and low-lifes, guarded only by two men, and one of them wounded.

"How's the arm?" McCutcheon asked Sampson.

"Hurting a little more now," Sampson admitted.

"Martinez will find you a doctor, I'm sure," McCutcheon replied.

"I'll be all right even if he doesn't," Sampson said. "It's just danged annoying, hurting this way."

They fell silent. Sampson was seated in a chair near the door, a rifle across his lap. He was rebinding his wounded arm with a rag bandage, but it was still bleeding, crimson starting to show through the fabric.

McCutcheon sat on a stool near the side window

that looked out onto the alleyway between the hotel and the next building. The other window in the room opened out over the wide main street, not a likely route of entrance for any would-be thief. But that side window made McCutcheon nervous, and he kept his eye on it.

"Wondering how Penn's doing?" he said.

"I'm concerned about him," Sampson said. "I don't think it's wise, him roaming out there alone. How does he expect to learn anything that way? He'll just get himself killed."

"What else could he have done, Jeff? Sit up in this room forever, hoping the kidnappers find us? Remember, right now the kidnappers probably know nothing about the massacre at the canyon, or that the original delivery plan has been knocked off course. They're probably waiting right now for that money to be delivered to them according to the terms of the original demand."

"Terms that we don't even know," Sampson said.

"Right . . . which is why Penn has to do what he's doing."

Sampson gently touched his wounded arm, winced, and took his hand away again. "I hope Bethany is all right."

"I do, too." McCutcheon shifted his position, allowing him to see out the window at a slightly sharper angle. He noted a window on the building across the alley. That window was slightly more elevated than the one through which he was looking. He discovered that he could use it as a sort of mirror, allowing him to see part of the flat rooftop area above their room. There was no one up there, which greatly relieved him. He'd fancied a time or two that he'd heard footsteps moving about above them.

McCutcheon scratched his right temple, keeping his eye on that reflecting window. "You know," he said,

"I've never seen Bethany Colby in person, but there was a portrait I saw through the window of Abel Blain's house."

"Yes," Sampson said. "That's her."

"She's a beauty, no question about it."

"The most beautiful lady I've ever known," Sampson said. "And that portrait hardly does her justice."

"Really? Because the picture alone was about enough to take a man's breath from him. What kind of lady is she?"

"Lively. Full of sparkle. Laughs a lot . . . breaks a lot of hearts."

"Including yours, maybe?"

Sampson gave a one-sided shrug, not moving the shoulder on his wounded side. "I'm just a common cowboy. Nobody she'd look twice at. She's got a lot better men than me to occupy her."

McCutcheon thought about that. "Any of those men seem the kind to carry her off for money?"

"I can't say. I know she's had suitors, but who they are, and what kind of men they are, I truly don't know." He frowned. "You think she might have been kidnapped by somebody she knows?"

"Oh, I don't know. Obviously it was somebody who knew her movements, and that she could be a potential source of money. It could be anyone, I suppose."

Sampson eyed the strongbox. "I wonder if paying that ransom is just going to cause Mr. Blain more problems down the road?"

"Maybe. But if I were him, I think I'd have done the same. You can't take a risk with the life of somebody you love. I think that—"

McCutcheon cut off abruptly and leaned forward, looking out the window.

"What is it, Jim?" Sampson asked.

"I think I saw something out there . . . maybe a reflection in that window. Somebody on the roof."

Sampson cocked his head, listening. "I don't hear anything up there."

McCutcheon stared at the window across the way, but it showed him nothing. But it reflected only a small area of the rooftop. And it was dark outside, making it difficult to be sure of any details that might be reflected in the dirty window glass.

McCutcheon pivoted. Sampson had heard it, too. Someone was moving stealthily down the hallway, from the sound of it. Then, immediately after, there was a faint thumping of footfalls above.

"Coming at us from two ways at once, maybe," McCutcheon whispered.

There was little light in the room; they burned only one lamp, and it was cranked down low.

Something bumped lightly against the wall outside the door, like an accidental touch.

Sampson came to his feet and made for the door as McCutcheon headed for the window.

Sampson, hardly aware of his painful wound, jerked the door open and lunged out into the hallway with his rifle leveled. He roared defiantly, just to keep up his own courage.

Two Mexican boys, perhaps thirteen yeas old, if that, yelled in horror and jumped back, falling all over themselves and winding up on their rumps.

They stared at Sampson's wild face, then at the rifle leveled at them. One promptly wet his trousers. The other pleaded in a high voice for his life.

Sampson's throat was constricted and he was having trouble breathing. His body and mind had catapulted into fighting mode when he heard the noise in the hallway, and it took him a few moments to reorient himself.

"Get up!" he barked in Spanish. "Go away from here, and don't come back."

They wept and thanked him, scrambling to their feet and running back down the hall toward the stairs. They descended so fast they almost fell over one another again.

Sampson slumped against the wall, drawing several deep breaths. He was sweating and drained. His arm began to hurt again.

For the moment, he'd forgotten Jim McCutcheon, and the noise they'd heard above.

After a moment, he reentered the room, just in time to see Jim McCutcheon, head thrust out the window, seemingly rise off the floor as if by some magic levitation, and move bodily toward the darkness outside.

Chapter Twenty-four

McCutcheon had reached the window about the time Sampson jerked open the door. He was determined not to be trapped in a purely defensive situation. If someone planned to enter this room from above, maybe by swinging through the window or simply shooting through the ceiling, McCutcheon didn't intend to wait for them.

He shoved the window up, still using the window across the alley as a mirror in which to view the roof above. But he could see nothing clearly. He studied the reflection in that window, but the roof appeared empty.

Yet he was sure he'd heard something, someone, up there.

He caught motion in the window . . . but not a reflection, he realized. The glass itself moved, the window beginning to go up.

McCutcheon leaned out his own window, his rifle extended and ready to fire. But the person who appeared in that opposite window was armed with nothing more than a crockery vessel.

It was a heavyset Mexican woman, with drooping, lazy eyes, who was simply emptying a chamber pot.

She looked up and saw McCutcheon. Those drooping eyes widened at the sight of the rifle. She screamed and pulled back inside, dropping the chamber pot. It plunged to the ground below and shattered.

McCutcheon winced, embarrassed, but thankful he'd not fired at her. He heard her high voice chattering wildly to someone else in the room with her.

A man appeared in her place at the window, cursing loudly in Spanish, shaking his fist at McCutcheon.

McCutcheon struggled to remember if he'd ever heard any words of apology in Spanish. With his head still thrust out the window, he tried to gesture in some manner to indicate he regretted his mistake.

He noticed, too late, that the man's expression had suddenly changed. The man was looking up now, above McCutcheon, toward the roof.

A loop of rope descended from above, encircled McCutcheon's neck, then jerked upward. Choking, he felt himself being pulled out the window. He dropped his rifle, which by good fortune fell back inside the room rather than falling to its ruination in the alley below.

McCutcheon grabbed at the rope, trying to loosen it from his neck. It was of no use. He managed to turn his head enough to look up and see that two men held the other end of it, up on top of the roof.

They must have hidden themselves behind the rise of the wall, which went up about a foot higher than the roof, during the time McCutcheon had been trying to see their reflection in the window across the alley.

McCutcheon felt someone grab his ankles. Sampson had him, and was pulling back, trying to keep him from being dragged fully out of the window.

Even as he choked and struggled, he wondered how this bizarre situation had managed to come about. The men must have planned to scale down to the window and enter the room. When he'd stuck his head out the window, they must have seen and seized the opportunity to remove one of the ransom money's guards in a most unexpected way.

McCutcheon managed to hook his feet below the

windowsill, allowing him to begin pulling back, along with Sampson. Then, amid bursting stars inside his brain and a blackness that seemed to be engulfing him, a though came: What if the men above let go of the rope? He'd plunge to the ground below, and possibly drag Sampson right out the window after him.

What happened, though, was not quite that. He gave a powerful pull with his legs just as Sampson also pulled back hard. He heard a yell of fright from above, and saw a body plunge over the edge of the roof and down.

The fellow had wrapped the rope around his hand to strengthen his pull. Too bad for him.

But it was also too bad for McCutcheon. The man's body fell past him, missing him by about an inch. The rope was still wound around the falling man's hand, and so, inevitably, McCutcheon was yanked hard when the slack gave out.

He was pulled from Sampson's grasp and out the window, falling through space into the dark alley below and landing, very hard, directly atop the man who had fallen from above him.

Sampson fell back onto his rump as McCutcheon's legs slipped from his grasp. Breathlessly he rose and looked out the window, down into the alley.

Above, he heard someone running across the roof—the second would-be intruder, the one who hadn't been pulled off the roof, was making his escape, whether to go below and check on the welfare of his unfortunate partner, or just to get away, Sampson could not know.

"Jim!" he called down from the window. "Jim! Are you okay?"

Apparently not. Though it was dark and hard to see details, he heard McCutcheon grunting . . . then the sound of someone running through the alley raggedly, as if somewhat injured.

Sampson pulled back inside, and ran out of the room, down the hallway and stairs, and through the lobby and outside.

He hardly noticed, as he passed them, the same two Mexican boys he'd run out of the hallway only a couple of minutes before. They were still loitering outside the hotel, and stepped back to let him pass.

Sampson rounded the corner of the building and entered the alley. McCutcheon was there, standing and dusting himself off, muttering some well-chosen curses beneath his breath.

"Jim, you're alive!"

"I landed on top of the other fellow. I guess he saved my life."

"Where is he?"

"Gone. He was hurt, I think, but managed to run off."

"I heard him from up in the window. But I didn't know whether it was him or you."

McCutcheon seemed disgusted. "Can you believe it? Getting roped and dragged out of your own danged window, nearly breaking your neck . . . what did they think they were going to do? Come down through the window?"

"Probably so." Sampson winced and touched his arm. "Blast it! All this thrashing around has got my wound to bleeding again."

"Remind me to feel sorry for you later. I could have died in that fall!"

Sampson said, "Good Lord . . . we'd best get back upstairs."

"The strongbox?"

"Unguarded."

Without another word, they ran back around the front of the hotel and through the door. McCutcheon and Sampson bolted up the stairs and to the open door of their room.

Sampson made it in first, McCutcheon right behind him. They both halted, speechless.

The strongbox was gone.

Across town, Jake Penn was standing in the shadows of an elevated wooden water tank, watching a possibly familiar figure entering a nearby cantina.

At least Penn thought he'd seen the fellow before. He couldn't attach a name to him, but his face was one Penn was nearly sure he'd seen squinting down at him over the barrel of a rifle aimed his way in the Gajardo Canyon.

If Penn was right, this sighting proved out what he'd expected would happen: Dresden and his gang had come to Castillo after the massacre at the canyon, counting on Jake Penn and his companions to bring the ransom money right to them.

The man who had just entered the cantina had been alone, and judging from his staggering and groping along, he was already somewhat drunk.

Penn wondered if there might be others of Dresden's gang inside that cantina. Maybe the Dresden brothers themselves were there.

There was only one way to know. He had to risk going in to take a look.

But what if he encountered Dresden, or some other member of that gang who could recognize him? What would happen? Penn realized that he himself might be subject to capture, and held subject to the release of the ransom. Bethany Colby could effectively be bypassed. Dresden and his brother would wind up with the money, and Bethany would remain hostage of her own kidnappers, with no ransom left to buy her freedom.

Penn was uncertain what to do, and didn't like the feeling. Uncertainty was mostly unfamiliar to him. For many years now he'd lived the life of a drifter, a man on the edges of society, rejected more often than not, sometimes merely because of the color of his skin. He'd grown accustomed to thinking on his feet, and staying on top of whatever situation he faced. His ability to always find a way out of whatever problem life threw him into was something he was aware of, and privately proud of.

This time he didn't feel proud. He'd managed to get the gold to Castillo, but now . . . what? He'd come out here to roam the town and somehow stumble upon a way to connect with Bethany's kidnappers. But it was surely a hopeless prospect.

This time, Penn's wit for survival seemed to be failing him.

He decided not to follow the man into the cantina. Too risky. Still, he would like to get a closer look, maybe see if Dresden was in that cantina, too. A glance through the window in the doorway shouldn't be too dangerous, he decided.

Penn headed for the cantina. Music poured from it, hammered out on an old piano. Up and down the street people moved, most of them seemingly revelers.

What a town! Penn wondered if it was this way every night. He heard the drunken shouts of men arguing from somewhere to the south. Shots followed. No one seemed to care, or even notice.

He reached the cantina door and cautiously eyed the interior through the window. He looked at the bar for the man he'd seen, but he wasn't there. Penn began to scan the entire room.

There he was! Seated at a table near the rear. Others were with him, but their backs were turned.

Penn couldn't be sure the man was one he'd seen at Gajardo Canyon. He'd only caught a glimpse. He strained to see the man better, and suddenly was jarred from behind.

"What the—"

He was caught in a small human wave as three men pushed into the cantina, crowding him along with them. He was turned about, almost knocked down, and by the time he caught himself, Penn was inside the cantina.

Chapter Twenty-five

Feeling exposed, Penn glanced toward the table where the man he'd been observing sat.

The man was talking to another beside him, not noticing Penn. Penn caught something odd about the fellow's expression, something in the way he cooly interacted with the man he was speaking with, the certain glassiness of his eyes.

Penn realized that this man was certainly not who he'd thought he was. This poor fellow could not possibly have been a Gajardo Canyon sniper: He was obviously blind.

Turning to leave, Penn experienced a mishap. By accident, his foot trod across the toes of a big, droop-jowled gringo who'd stretched back in his chair at just the wrong time.

"Beg your pardon, friend," Penn said. "I didn't mean to do that."

The big man, who looked quite stupid, glared up at him. Penn touched the brim of his hat and tried to look apologetic.

Another figure suddenly loomed before him. The drinking partner of the man whose toes he'd just trodden had risen and blocked him from the door.

"You just stepped on my brother's foot, boy," the man said. He was very close to Penn and his breath was nothing to savor.

"I'm mighty sorry," Penn said. "It was clumsy of me, and I apologize."

"Well! Listen at you! You don't sound like most darkies I know. You talk real smooth, boy."

"Sir, I'm truly sorry about what I did. It wasn't by intention."

The man abruptly shoved Penn against the chest, making him stagger back. Inevitably, he bumped up against the man he'd already trodden upon.

"There! You done it again!"

Marvelous, Penn thought. *A drunk fool looking for trouble is just what I need right now.*

"I couldn't much help it then, sir," Penn said. "You pushed me back against him."

The man grinned evilly, and reached under his coat. He came out with a gleaming knife.

"Going to cut you, boy," he said. "Going to collect me a colored man's ear tonight! I've always wanted me one!"

Penn was not seriously afraid of this fellow. That knife would never touch his flesh; Penn wouldn't allow it. He could see any of a dozen ways of taking this man down where he stood. But a row with this fool would probably only cause trouble with others, and trouble was not what he needed to find tonight.

"Mister, let me buy you and your brother a drink," he said. "Just to show there's no hard feelings."

The fellow softened just a little. "A drink?"

"Yes, sir. Whatever you want. I'll pay for it out of my own pocket."

The man pondered half a second, then shook his head. "I can buy me my own drink. Bet you there's cantinas in this town where I could trade a colored man's ear for a whole bottle, matter of fact!"

Others were beginning to pick up on what was going on, and they were clearly enjoying it. Penn glanced around and realized how unwelcome he was here.

Probably few blacks were ever seen in this little Mexican town, and clearly, there was no friendly spirit here toward his race.

He glanced behind him and noted a rear door. It would do nothing for his pride to flee, but Penn was smart enough to know that pride can kill.

"I'll be going now, sir," he said to the man with the knife. And before the liquor-slowed fellow could react, he moved quickly for that rear doorway.

Someone tripped him before he could get there. Penn fell down hard, then sensed that he was in danger and rolled to the side just as a heavy, thudding sound filled his ear.

The man with the knife had followed him and tried to stomp his head while he was down.

Penn got mad. He sprang to his feet with an agility and celerity that roused a couple of whoops of admiration from some of the watching men. A Mexican saloon girl chattered something that drew laughter, and Penn go the idea that the joke, whatever it was, had not been on him, but on his staggering opponent.

The man swung the knife in a wide, clumsy arc. Penn's hand shot out, grabbed the man's wrist, and twisted. The knife fell from the man's hand, and before it could hit the ground, Penn kicked it up and away. It flashed across the room and stuck into the far wall.

What a stroke of luck! Penn couldn't possibly have pulled off a trick like that by design. But it looked like he had, and the slick move generated a burst of applause and howls of approval.

"Ready for me to buy you that drink now?" Penn asked the stunned man whose wrist he still held.

The man cursed and struck at him with his other fist. Penn dodged the blow and twisted his wrist some more, causing the man to bellow in pain.

The stupid-looking partner of Penn's victim stumbled up swinging.

Penn ducked the blows, stomped the man's foot again, then brought up a knee that caught him in the groin. The man made a pitiful noise and doubled over. Penn shoved him down with his foot.

With a deft turn, he twisted the wrist of the former knife-bearer in the opposite direction, causing the fellow to scream and drop to his knees as the bones in his wrist nearly came apart.

"I asked you if you were ready for that drink now!" Penn said to him firmly.

"Yes!" the man said. "Yes! Just let go of my arm! It's about to snap!"

Penn let him go. The man stumbled off, gingerly holding his wrist.

"Give them whatever they want," Penn said to the barkeep. He flipped a couple of coins over the bar and headed for that back door.

Somebody slapped him on the shoulder goodnaturedly, and he heard various exclamations of admiration in both English and Spanish. He'd earned himself some much-needed respect just now.

But he also earned a lot of attention. Was it a good thing? He wasn't sure. He knew it was no secret that ransom money was being transported from the Blain ranch into Mexico. And Dresden and his gang, at least, knew that the money was in the custody of Jake Penn, who because of his race stood out here like a tombstone in a tea parlor.

If word of this altercation spread, Dresden would probably know, if he didn't know already, that Jake Penn and the ransom were now in Castillo. And he'd come looking.

On the other hand, Penn wondered if the kidnappers of Bethany Colby also knew that the ransom was in the custody of a black man. If they did, then drawing attention to himself might prove a good thing, if it made them seek him out. Those were the only men in this town whom he wanted to find him.

Penn left through the rear door and headed into the back alleys of Castillo.

No one followed him. He wound his way this way and that, trying to lose himself. Those men whom he'd humiliated would soon regain their courage and probably want to regain their pride, too. They might come after him, and just now he simply didn't have the time or available attention to devote to them.

Five minutes later, Penn rounded the rear of another building and headed up one last alley toward the main street. He was worrying again, wondering how in the devil he was supposed to learn the details of the ransom delivery process without advertising to all the wicked world that half a million dollars was now in Castillo, kept in nothing more secure than a hotel room, overseen only by two very weary men.

He almost stumbled over something in the alley. He stopped and looked down at it, thinking it was a box or a crate, then dropped to his knees to examine it.

It wasn't a crate. It was a strongbox. The lock was blasted to pieces and the top lay open.

And the strongbox was empty.

Penn stared at the empty strongbox and began to feel ill.

How would he get Bethany Colby back now?

He studied the box. It seemed miscolored, as if something had spilled on it.

Picking it up, he carried it toward the front of the alley, where light splayed into the entrance from a side window of a dance hall. Indeed, this appeared to be the strongbox they'd been guarding. And there was dried blood on it.

Penn began to breathe faster. Blood implied violence, wounding. Dried blood implied it had happened sometime back.

This box must have been stolen from the hotel almost immediately after he left the room. And there must have been a fight of some kind, and someone hurt badly enough to bleed rather heavily onto the strongbox.

He should never have left. He'd abandoned his companions for a fool's errand, wandering the streets in the vain hope that he'd stumble upon Bethany Colby's kidnappers by sheer chance.

Just now, Jake Penn felt like he ought to just shoot himself and be done with it. He deserved nothing better.

He put the ruined strongbox under his arm and headed for the street, planning to run back to the hotel.

Chapter Twenty-six

A figure, clad in ragged clothing that seemed to have no specific shape or pattern, appeared before Penn.

"Where you going with that!" a rather high-pitched voice challenged. "That's *my* box."

Penn had dealt with the men at the cantina without breaking a sweat, but for some reason this short, strange creature, shrouded in rags and darkness, unnerved him.

"What? *Your* box?"

"That's right! Give it back!"

Penn realized just then part of what was unsettling about this being. The general appearance was that of a man, but the voice seemed to be a woman's. He truly couldn't tell the sex of this stranger. All he could be sure of was that this was no Mexican. Just one more displaced Yankee who'd wandered south of the border for whatever reason—probably reasons best left unknown, if this person's history was typical of most such expatriates.

"Where did you get this box?" Penn demanded. "Did you take this from a hotel room?"

"Hotel room? I didn't take that from no such! I *found* it, I did!"

"Empty?"

"It *is* empty! Are you so much a fool you can't tell

an empty box from a full one? But it's *mine!* You give it back!"

Penn shook his head. "This isn't your box. It was taken from me and some friends of mine, and something important was taken out of it. Do you know what happened to what was in this box?"

"They's nothing in that box! Nothing but breathing air! Give me it back!"

Completely loco, Penn thought. *Maybe dangerous, if he, or she, is armed.*

"Can't keep nothing no more!" the strange being whined. "Got so you can't have nothing without somebody stealing it from you!"

Tell me about it, Penn thought. "I'll buy it from you," he said.

The other froze. "How much?"

Penn pulled out a dollar bill and held it out. The other person stared at it, then suddenly lunged forward and snatched it away.

"Just an old box! Just an old busted strongbox, and you give me a dollar for it! Ha!"

Penn couldn't care less about the ridicule of a crazed vagrant. He turned and carried the strongbox away, heading for the hotel.

He wanted to make sure this was, in fact, the same strongbox they'd carried from the Blain ranch. And he wanted to know how that blood had gotten on it, and whose it was.

One thing was certain, Penn considered as he made his way back to the hotel. The one who had sold him the box wasn't the same one who had taken it. Whoever had taken it was half a million dollars richer right now. If the vagrant had taken the strongbox, that dollar Penn had offered wouldn't have been at all tempting.

Penn reached the hotel and stormed through the lobby, almost bowling over a man who was exiting.

The man protested in Spanish, and Penn muttered an apology in English, and continued up the stairs.

The door to their room was open, a dim light still burning inside the room. Penn entered. The room was empty.

He dropped the strongbox and felt very disturbed. What had happened to McCutcheon and Sampson? He should have never left them alone.

Best to be sure of the facts before drawing a conclusion, Penn thought to himself as he closed the door and cranked up the lamp, brightening the room. His hands trembled as he turned the wick screw.

Tossing his hat onto the bed, he sat down before the strongbox and looked closely at the blood on it. He flicked at it with a fingernail. It was quite dry, very crusty. This blood had been on the box for quite some time.

A flicker of hope rose. If the blood were McCutcheon's or Sampson's, it would be much fresher.

Penn then began to examine it more closely, holding the lamp near and letting its light bathe over the box. The closer he looked, the less certain he was that this was the same strongbox they had guarded. When he looked at the hinges, he realized that it certainly was a different box. He'd chanced to take note of the hinge shape on the original strongbox. Those hinges were square and blunt. These were much longer, and oval.

He closed his eyes for a moment and drew in one more deep, cleansing breath. Maybe the original strongbox wasn't missing at all. Maybe McCutcheon and Sampson had taken it elsewhere for some reason, and were still guarding it.

But if so, where? And why? They'd been under strict orders to guard that strongbox and not let it out of this room. Surely they hadn't done so without compelling reason.

He couldn't help but assume the worst. But to go out searching for them didn't seem to be a promising approach. He could scour this ever-moving little town for hours and not locate them, especially at night.

Maybe they'd return. Maybe they'd been forced to leave the room for some good but innocuous reason, and had taken the strongbox with them.

He'd wait for a time, as long as he could stand it. It would be bad if they should return only to find him not here.

He sat on the bed and stared at the door. He wasn't sure he'd ever been so tired, or so worried, in his life.

Sampson and McCutcheon were moving about the town with the furtive, helpless manner of two scared rats searching for some lost scrap of food.

"It was those boys," Sampson said. "I'm sure of it. I think I passed them while I was running around to the alley to see if you were all right. They must have taken the strongbox while we were both in the alley."

McCutcheon looked around as if hoping the thieves would simply show themselves in the open street. He knew they were probably well hidden somewhere by now. He cursed the nighttime gloom.

"I don't know what to do," he admitted. "I wish Penn was here."

"What could he do any better than us?"

"Maybe nothing. But Penn usually has a way of dealing with whatever comes up."

"He's not going to be happy about us losing that strongbox. Especially to a couple of common street muchacos."

"We've got to find it. There's just no other option. If we don't, Bethany Colby has no chance at all."

"Should we split up and cover more ground?"

McCutcheon considered it very briefly, then shook his head. "No. With two of us there's a better chance we'll be able to take it back together if we do find it. Whoever has it, those boys or anybody else, isn't going to want to part with it."

"I hope it's the boys, then. We'd stand a better chance against them."

"Were they armed?"

"I don't think so."

"Come on. Let's keep looking, maybe over at that livery stable. Having that amount of money might put somebody in the mind of trying to ride out of this town as fast as possible."

They moved off together.

PART III

Showdown

Chapter Twenty-seven

Martinez was relieved. He'd been certain that someone was following him in the shadows around the walled church, but apparently he'd been wrong. He'd darted behind a tree and awaited whomever had been behind him. No one ever appeared. They'd merely turned off in a new direction.

Even so, he'd found a couple of low-hanging limbs on a nearby tree and gone over the wall into the churchyard at the first opportunity. Once inside, he felt much safer. Holy places had always given him a feeling of protection, at the same time filling him with a certain awe.

He looked about the dark churchyard, noting the blackness of each visible window, and realizing how late the hour was. The priest would surely be asleep.

But a glimmer of light caught his eye, spilling out around the edges of a closed shutter of a small annex built onto the end of the church. He headed in that direction.

His intention was to peer around the shutter to see if the priest was still up, but even before he reached the window a door opened and the priest emerged, a lamp in his hand. He looked at his visitor with heavily lined, weary, yet penetrating black eyes.

"Hello, my friend. God bless you this night. Have you come to see me?"

Martinez felt compelled to warn this good man

about his lack of caution in emerging to meet a stranger in so rough and violent a town. "You should be more careful, Father. I might be a thief."

The priest laughed. "Oh, my friend, do I not know the dangers of this town, after so many years here? I am here to serve God. He will protect me, if He wills, or otherwise take me to be with Him. So either way, I have no cause to fear. My name is Father Mateo. How may I help you?"

"I am Luis Martinez. I'm told you are like a doctor in this town."

Father Mateo's smile seemed sad. He sighed. "It's as I expected. Many people come to me for physical healing. Very few indeed seem to worry about their own souls. But no matter. I'll help you if I can."

"It's not me, Father. There is a man I've come to town with, a gringo, who was wounded in the arm by a bullet."

"Your friend is a violent man, then. It's usually men who live by the gun who end up wounded by the same."

"Not this time. This is not a violent man. He is good, and on a mission that is very important. You could call it a holy mission, Father—the salvation of a young woman who is in great danger." He paused. Surely this priest could be trusted. "She is the daughter of a rich man in Texas, and she has been kidnapped."

Father Mateo's dark eyes narrowed. "The Blain ranch kidnapping?"

Martinez was chilled. It was one thing for the story of ransom money to be whispered about among the kind of human vermin who frequented the border country, but for some reason he hadn't really expected the priest to know about it. For a moment he was distrustful, but corrected himself. This was a priest, after all. A man of God.

"So the ransom money is here in Castillo? At this moment?" the priest asked.

Martinez again felt suspicious, but again reminded himself to whom he was speaking. "Yes. Guarded in the hotel by only two men, one of them wounded. That's why I've come to fetch you. I want to take you to him so you can treat his wound." Martinez paused. "Perhaps you can also say a prayer for us, to protect us while we have the money in our possession. There are many men who have already tried to steal it from us."

The priest shook his head. "I can't go to your friend. There is another man here who is very badly hurt. It's because I've been treating his wounds that I'm awake at this late hour. I fear he'll die soon, despite what I've done. So you must bring your wounded friend here. And the money, as well. It will be safer here than anywhere else in this town."

"How is it you have come to know about this kidnapping, Father Mateo?"

The priest looked solemnly at him. "A priest hears many things. Some of them he is not free to share— even when he wishes he could." He paused, seemingly weighing his words. "It may be, though, that there is another who can speak when I can't."

Martinez was puzzled by this cryptic talk. Again he felt a flash of mistrust, and again he squelched it. He'd been taught to always revere the priesthood.

Father Mateo took a step nearer and held up the lamp, letting its light illuminate his face and reveal the striking intensity of his expression. "You must bring the money here. It is very important. You have not come here by chance, my friend. God has surely sent you to me, because this town is a place of great danger for you. There are things I know, but can't share with you. Not yet, anyway."

Martinez frowned. All this was quite unexpected,

and very strange. For silent moments he stared at the priest, who lowered the lamp. The changing pattern of light and shadow on his face masked the keenness of his expression as he repeated, "You must bring the money here. You are in great danger in this town, my friend. Perhaps even more than you know."

Penn could stand it no longer. Wise or not, he couldn't just stay here waiting for God only knew what to happen. He had to leave the hotel and go find the others.

He checked his weapons, said a fast, fervent prayer, and headed out the door, closing it behind him.

He was halfway down the hall when he heard footsteps on the stairs. Penn paused, stepping back. Every noise in this town, every shadow, filled him with caution.

But he stepped forward again when he saw who had come up the stairs.

"Jim!" he declared to McCutcheon. "You look pale as a ghost . . . and you the same, Jeff. And the strongbox—where is it?"

"It's gone, Jake," McCutcheon said. "If I look pale, that's the reason. All the money . . . gone. We've failed in the worst way. There was trouble—I took a fall out the window, into the alley. Jeff ran down to help me, and when we got back—"

"A fall out the window?"

"It's a strange story, I admit. I'm lucky to have survived. I can tell you the tale right now, if you want . . . but the end of it is that the money is gone, and we can't find it."

"Who do you think took it?"

"Maybe a couple of boys who were hanging around close by. But we don't know. It could have been Martinez, I suppose."

Penn thought about that and shook his head. "No.

No. My instinct tells me different about that. Martinez can be trusted. I'm sure of it. Have you seen him since he went doctor-searching?"

"No. What about you? Did you find out where to take the ransom . . . not that it matters now, considering the ransom is gone."

"I didn't learn a thing," Penn admitted. "And I have no clue as to how we ever *will* learn a thing. But you're right: Without the money, it doesn't matter anyway. We've got to find it. Jim, answer me something: That strongbox did have square hinges on it, didn't it?"

"I don't know . . . why do you ask that?"

"I found another strongbox out on the street, broken open. At first I thought it was ours, but when I got it back up here, the hinges were rounded, and ours were square, I feel sure."

"That's right," Sampson said. "They were square."

"There was blood on that strongbox I found," Penn threw in.

"Blood? From who?"

"I don't know. I suppose I shouldn't be surprised. I suspect there's a lot of bloodshed in a town like this. But forget that. What we've got to do now is find that ransom money."

"I don't think it's any use," McCutcheon answered. "We've been looking all over, and had no luck."

"Well, there's three to look now," Penn said. "Let's give it another try—give it all the tries necessary. There's a young woman's life at stake if we fail."

They headed down the stairs together, passing through the lobby and out onto the dark street.

Chapter Twenty-eight

The three desperate men searched the town, growing more hopeless with every minute that passed.

"It's no use, I'm afraid," Penn said. "That strongbox probably isn't even in town now. Somebody's taken it out onto the plains, sure as anything. They've probably busted it open and are rolling in money right now."

"What's going to happen to Bethany now?" Sampson asked.

"I don't like to think about that," Penn said.

"But we do have a strongbox," McCutcheon said.

"What good is that, without money?"

"Maybe we can close it up, stuff it full of something, and make the kidnappers think there's money in it."

Penn shook his head. "They'd have to be mighty foolish to fall for such a trick as that. We'd just get Bethany killed, and us along with her." Penn paused. "There's only one thing to do, gents. We're going to have to find those kidnappers and tell them what's happened. We'll have to see if we can buy more time. Then we're going to have to go back to Abel, and see if he can round up the same ransom again."

"Another half-million dollars?" Sampson said. "Mr. Blain is rich, but not rich enough to do that."

"What else can we do, though?" Penn asked.

"We've botched this thing up mighty bad," McCutcheon threw in.

Penn didn't like to hear that, but he knew McCutcheon was right. "There was failure built into this from the beginning," he replied. "The kidnappers themselves guaranteed it. It wasn't very smart on their part to demand the ransom to be carried all the way to Castillo. Too many chances for failure, and for discovery."

"An amateur job, then," McCutcheon said.

Penn pondered that. "Yes. Yes. I'll bet you whoever kidnapped Bethany is no experienced criminal."

"So maybe they ain't so smart we can't fool them," McCutcheon said. "We may have no other choice, Penn."

Penn didn't reply. He was staring across the street. Lifting his hand, he pointed at the entrance to an alleyway. "There's where I found the strongbox," he said.

"Let's go take another look over there," Sampson said. "Maybe we'll get lucky and find the *right* strongbox this time."

There was no reason not to give it a try, so they strode across the street and into the alley. There was, of course, no miraculous discovery of the missing money.

But there was still the odd person from whom Penn had purchased the damaged strongbox. The figure rose from behind a barrel so fast that Sampson and McCutcheon were startled. Sampson actually went for his gun.

"Hold up, there, Jeff," Penn said. "This fellow won't hurt you."

"Fellow!" the figure declared. "Why you calling me that? Don't you know a woman when you see one?"

So that mystery was solved.

"I beg your pardon, ma'am. I should have realized," Penn said.

"Ah, I know you!" she said. "You're the one who bought my box from me!"

"That's right. Good evening to you, ma'am. We'll leave you be."

"Wait a minute," Sampson said. "Ma'am, might you step over here, closer to this window?"

The woman backed away, instantly wary. "What you want from me?"

"I just want to see that shawl you've got on, ma'am."

Indeed, she was wearing one. She hadn't had one on when Penn had seen her before.

"You don't get my shawl! It's *mine!*"

"I just want to see it, ma'am. I'll pay you a dollar just to see it."

Those were words she would listen to. "Well! Let's see that dollar, then."

He produced it, and handed it to her. She stepped up, into the light of the nearby window, with the air of a society woman showing off her finery.

"What's your interest in that, Jeff?" Penn asked.

"I know that shawl," Sampson replied, is voice tight. "It belongs to Bethany Colby."

The news was so stunning that no one replied for a few moments.

"Wait a minute," McCutcheon said. "How can you be sure?"

"I gave Bethany that shawl," Sampson replied. He sounded like he might be on the verge of tears. "I gave it to her without her ever knowing it was from me. I was . . . shy about it. I sent it to her without my name on it."

"Jeff, it's likely just another shawl that looks like the one you gave her," Penn said.

"No," Sampson replied. "There's her initials, stitched into the corner. I did that myself."

Penn stepped up close and held up a corner of the

shawl. Sure enough, the initials "BC" were embroidered into a corner.

"Sell it to you . . . three dollars!" the woman declared, one eye squinting, the other glaring.

"I'll take that bargain, ma'am," Penn said, digging for money. "But on one condition: Tell us how, and where, and when, you came by this shawl."

She wouldn't answer until the money was in hand. Penn took the shawl, then handed it to Sampson, who held it tenderly, staring at it and clearly struggling with welling emotions.

"There's dried blood on it . . . right here," he said softly.

"Tell me about the shawl, ma'am," Penn asked again.

"Got it the same place and same time as the busted box. The place where the dead men are."

"I don't understand, Jake," McCutcheon said. "This doesn't make sense. Her shawl, with blood on it, a broken strongbox . . . and dead men? What does it mean?"

Penn shook his head. "I don't know. I really don't."

Luis Martinez trotted through the dark town toward the hotel, eager to fetch his companions back to the safety of the church. The things Father Mateo had said had roused his curiosity. There was something important to be learned at that church, but the priest wasn't going to present it until the others were there.

Martinez came into view of the hotel and glanced up toward the window. A light burned there dimly. This was as Martinez expected; he had no way to know the things that had transpired since he'd been sent out to find a doctor.

A movement at the window made him glance up again. He saw a man there, looking out across the street.

It was only a flash. The person's face hadn't really been visible. Yet Martinez felt nearly certain that the person in the room was not one of his companions.

Someone else was up there. But who? And where were McCutcheon, Sampson, Penn?

He slipped into a recessed doorway, thinking hard. He wasn't about to go up to the hotel room without knowing what was going on. For all he knew, his three companions were killed, and the ransom stolen. Maybe the man he'd seen in the window had known that there was one more who had checked into this room. Maybe the stranger in the room was waiting for the last ransom rider to return, and then get rid of him.

On the other hand, maybe it was all a great mistake. Maybe his eyes had fooled him, and the figure in the window had been McCutcheon, or Sampson.

Not being sure, Martinez simply stayed where he was, the scales equally balanced, giving him no grounds for decision.

All at once, he was angry. This was absurd! Why was he even here? This was none of his affair! Let the two gringos and the negro deal with this situation. He'd already endangered himself for them enough, even killed that sniper in the grove to protect them!

At this moment, Martinez honestly couldn't say what had compelled him to join them. Surely it had been a kind of madness born of grief over his dead father.

He would go to the stable, get his horse, and ride away from this town. Right away.

He left the doorway and aimed himself in the direction of the livery.

He rounded the rear of a store along the way, and heard a thumping, rattling noise, followed by a boy's voice, cursing. More thumping of something metallic ensued, followed by more cursing.

Curiosity drew Martinez. He paused and looked

into the shadowed area from whence the noises and voice proceeded.

Martinez saw there two Mexican boys kneeling beside a box of some sort, hammering on it with a stone. They were engrossed in their effort, which was obviously frustrating them in some way, and did not notice him.

He looked at the box.

It was a strongbox. The one that held the ransom.

Martinez drew his pistol and clicked back the hammer. Then he leveled it at the boys.

"Go away!" he ordered fiercely. "Leave here, now!"

They came to their feet, stumbling about and very surprised. They did not argue, though, considering the pistol aimed at them.

One of them stooped to pick up the strongbox on the slender chance that this man was ordering them away for some territorial reason, not to get his own hands on the box.

"No!" Martinez commanded. "Leave the box!"

"Sir," one of the boys said, "it's ours. It's important to us. You must let us keep it!"

"It's stolen!" Martinez said. "It's not yours! Go away, or I'll shoot you!"

With last, longing glances at the strongbox, which was now damaged by their pounding, the boys turned and departed into the darkness. Martinez waited a moment, then roared and ran after them. Sure enough, they'd stopped as soon as they were sufficiently deep in the shadows to not be seen. His run at them, though, scared them into a more thorough flight this time.

Martinez holstered his pistol, went to the strongbox, and picked it up. Settling it on his shoulder, he headed for the hotel.

By the time he was near the hotel, he'd managed

to think through some of the implications of finding
the strongbox in the possession of strangers, and well
away from the hotel.

Clearly the box had been stolen. But that couldn't
have happened without some sort of trickery or violence against McCutcheon and Sampson, who had
guarded it. But could these boys have managed to do
that? They weren't even armed.

What of the figure he'd seen at the hotel window?
The one he did not believe had been any of his prior
companions? Might that be the true thief? If so, why
would he linger in the hotel room while common
street boys made off with the strongbox?

Martinez wasn't sure what to make of it all. He was
rendered cautious, though, and decided not to simply
walk back into the hotel without looking over the situation first.

He found a hiding place between buildings within
view of the hotel, and sat the strongbox down at his
feet.

But he never looked at the hotel. Martinez stared
at the box instead, thinking about the money in it. An
incredible amount of money. Inconceivable. And right
there before him, easy to pick up and simply carry
away.

His throat went dry all at once. He swallowed hard,
starting to shake now. New and intriguing—and fright-
ening—possibilities were beginning to play through
his mind.

He thought of the life of poverty he'd lived. The
times he'd longed for something beyond the squalor
and want.

It would be so easy.

Martinez played it out in his mind. Pick up the box.
Carry it to the livery stable. Strap it onto his horse.
Then ride away.

Could he do it? His heart hammered. He was beginning to tremble harder.

He stooped and picked up the strongbox, and hefted it onto his shoulder. Settling it in place, he looked around furtively, and began to walk.

Chapter Twenty-nine

Penn stepped toward the woman in the alley, his movement so quick it startled her. She backed away from him.

"Tell me about the place where the dead men are," he said. "Tell me what that means."

"Men was killed . . ." she said. "I found the box, and the shawl. That's all."

"Do you know why these men were killed?"

Penn's intense manner was scaring her. She didn't answer, but stepped back some more.

"Please, ma'am. Don't run away."

She turned, then ran away.

"Penn, should I—"

"No, Jim. Let her go. I don't think there's more she can tell us."

"Penn, you've figured something out here."

"No . . . maybe. I don't know."

Sampson touched his wounded arm lightly, wincing.

"Hurts worse," he said. "And I'm cold."

"There's a fire over yonder," McCutcheon said. "See it?"

Someone had built then abandoned a bonfire over in an empty lot on the other side of the street. It was nearly burned out now.

"Let's go warm ourselves and think a bit," Penn said.

There was some more scrap wood nearby. Penn fed

the flames and they sat around the fire. Penn stared into the flames, against his usual practice, not caring like he usually did that he would be momentarily blinded when he looked next into the darkness. He had much to think about right now.

"Penn, what is it you've figured out?" McCutcheon asked.

"Let me ask you some questions," Penn replied. "Imagine, for now, that you're Keith Dresden and his brother. You've decided to betray Abel Blain, and Bethany Colby, for the sake of getting your hands on a strongbox with half a million dollars in it. You've gone so far as to murder six men just to get the money for yourself, but the money has disappeared on you, and you don't know whether it's buried under a rock-slide or carried off. Now, imagine you've come ahead to this town, in hopes that the ransom will be brought in on your heels, and you can—you hope—get it back. Tell me: What would your biggest fear be in that situation?"

McCutcheon pondered a moment. "I suppose that the money would be stolen before I could get it."

"Right. Or barring that, what else?"

Sampson answered this time. "That the people with the money would get the money to the kidnappers too fast for you to get it yourself."

"Absolutely," Penn said. "Exactly right. So what might you do in such a set of circumstances?"

McCutcheon said, "Penn, I'm tired. Forget the questions and just tell us the answers."

"All right. Here's what you'd do. If you were Dresden and his hired men, you'd have one advantage that the men with the ransom—namely us—wouldn't have."

Sampson was following Penn's track more easily than McCutcheon was. "Dresden knows exactly where the ransom was to be delivered!" he said.

"Right. And where the ransom was to be taken is

the very last thing that Dresden would want *us* to
know. Because we just might succeed in getting that
ransom delivered, you see, and if that happened, Dresden would likely lose any chance at getting it."

"All right," McCutcheon said. "All that's obvious
enough. But what are you trying to get at?"

"Let's take a look at what we've stumbled across.
A strongbox, empty and broken open. There's blood
on it. A shawl that we know is Bethany's. Blood on
that, too. And both the box and the shawl found by
a woman who talks about the place where the 'dead
men' are."

"Dear Lord!" Sampson exclaimed after a few moments' thought.

Penn nodded. "I think you just grasped what I'm
getting at, son."

"Dresden and his brother got themselves a strongbox of their own, and delivered it to the kidnappers!"

"Yep. And then, I'm willing to bet, they did to those
kidnappers what they'd already done to the ransom
bearers in Gajardo Canyon. Delivered to them an empty
strongbox, lured the kidnappers into position . . . and
gunned them down. Remember the blood on the
strongbox?"

"And blood on the shawl," Sampson said.

"Yes."

"But what about Bethany?"

"I don't know. We have to consider that she could
have been killed, either by the original kidnappers or
by Dresden and his gang. If not, I suspect that she's
still a hostage, but this time, a hostage of Dresden and
his brother, not whoever originally took her."

McCutcheon said, "Jake, you're trying to weave
cloth from spiderwebs. Piecing together a lot of stray
facts that may not have anything to do with one
another."

"But the *shawl,* Jim. The shawl. Somehow, Bethany

Colby's shawl was found along with the empty strong-box. Whatever happened there, whoever was killed, Bethany was there."

Sampson groaned softly, touching his wounded arm.

"We're going to have to find you help on our own, it appears, Jeff," Penn said. "I don't know that we'll see Martinez again. Come on. Let's go find somebody to patch you up."

They left the fire and walked through the town. Every cantina was busy, every alleyway and shadowed recess filled with barely seen people who lurked like ghosts.

"This town is surely a haven for the damned," Penn said.

A boy darted past. Penn accosted him. "Amigo!"

The boy stopped and faced them. *"Sí?"*

"Ask him, Jeff."

Sampson, in a voice tight with pain and with blood oozing between his fingers as he gripped his arm, asked the boy where he might find medical care. The boy chattered an answer.

"He says there's a priest who tends to the sick. There is no doctor other than him," Sampson translated.

Penn pointed at the dark tower of the church. *"Iglesia?"*

The boy nodded. Penn gave him a coin, which was gratefully received.

"Fellows, let's go stir a priest out of his bed," Penn said. "Maybe while he's patching you up, Jeff, I can confess to him just how bad a job I've done of trying to lead our little mission tonight. It ain't your ordinary night that I let half a million dollars in ransom money slip between my fingers." He paused. "And maybe I can get him to pray for Bethany. I expect she needs it."

They reached the wall around the church. Not immediately finding a gate, they helped one another to simply climb over it.

"There's a light burning in a window over there," McCutcheon pointed out.

They headed for the light. Penn, for some reason, felt oddly alarmed all at once. He stopped, looking around, instinctively expecting trouble. His hand crept toward his pistol.

A door nearby burst open suddenly, and a dark figure lunged out threateningly, right for them.

Chapter Thirty

Penn had his pistol drawn and cocked by the time he realized that the advancing figure was familiar.

"Martinez!" he exclaimed. "Dear Lord, man, I might have shot you!" In the emotion of the moment, it didn't cross Penn's mind that Martinez could not understand him.

Nor, apparently, did Martinez consider the fact that Penn could not understand him. He was chattering with excitement, not evidently concerned that Penn had just drawn a pistol on him.

"What's he saying, Jeff?" Penn asked.

"He says that the money is here!" Sampson replied in a tone of surprise. "And something about a wounded man who the priest wants us to meet."

"Priest? The priest hasn't even met us yet."

As if cued by the comment, a figure passed the inside of the lighted window. A door opened, and Mateo emerged.

"I am Father Mateo," he said in Spanish. "Who are you?"

Martinez turned and began excitedly talking, leaving no opening for anyone else to respond to the priest.

"He asked who we are," Sampson translated. "His own name is Matthew . . . Mateo, in his tongue."

The priest looked past the chattering Martinez and said, "You speak English, I presume?" His own English was remarkably precise and clear.

"Yes," Penn replied.

"I know who you are," Mateo said. "Your good friend here, Martinez, has told me about you and your mission. It is truly the hand of God that has brought you to me tonight. Martinez tried to find you and bring you here but couldn't. Now you've come to us on your own. God is truly guiding you. And that's good, because there is much for you to fear."

"I'm puzzled, Father," Penn said. "We came here only because we were told you could tend to wounds, not because of any divine leading that I could see. My friend here, Jeff Sampson, has been wounded in the arm, and needs bandaging. My name is Penn, by the way. Jake Penn. This other fellow here is my partner, Jim McCutcheon."

"The hand of God sometimes leads with a light touch," Mateo said. "And He leads those who are doing His work, whether they perceive it clearly at the time or not. And you are doing His work, for you bear the ransom to free the poor kidnapped girl."

"We did bear it . . . but we lost it. Did I understand that the money—"

"Is here. Yes. Again, the hand of God. It is astonishing that Martinez was able to find it and bring it safely here. It had been stolen, he said, by two boys."

Penn was so amazed he couldn't reply. Indeed it did seem that no less than a divine hand could have brought such a stroke of fortune. The ransom was safe after all! He looked with deep admiration at Martinez, who had at last quit talking and now stood grinning behind the priest. Rather than steal the money for himself, Martinez evidently had recovered it and brought it here for safekeeping. It seemed no less than a miracle.

"I will tend to your wounds, my son," Mateo said to Sampson. "But I will do it quickly. There is a man who is prepared to speak to you and tell you the truth about the kidnapping, and what has happened to the poor Blain girl. You must hear him quickly though. His time in this world is short."

"I don't understand," Penn said.

"You will, soon enough," the priest replied. "Come now. Let's go inside and see how bad this wound is."

In fact, the wound wasn't really particularly bad. Sampson had a nice furrow gouged through his bicep, causing great pain and quite a lot of bleeding when he moved, but nothing had lodged in the wound and the priest was able to clean and bandage it with dispatch.

Penn watched Mateo at his work and admired the man. What a thankless job it surely must be to attempt to give spiritual guidance in a town in which the only spirit that mattered was that in a bottle, and in which lust and violence were the only objects of widespread worship.

"Now, come," Mateo said. "Meet a man who told me in confession the things you need to know. I can't share myself what is told to me in confession, but he can tell you, and has agreed to do so. If his strength fails him before he can finish, he has given me permission to tell you the rest."

"Who are you talking about?" Penn said.

"In here," Mateo replied. "Come and meet him."

He led them into an adjacent room. There, lying on a bed, bathed in candlelight, was the bandage-swathed form of a young man who had evidently suffered multiple wounds. He was a white man, dark-haired, well-featured. He didn't appear to be moving, and Mateo rushed to his side. He was breathing, after all, but lightly.

A sense of imminent death was strong in the room, almost like a stench.

"My son," Mateo said. "They have come. Will you still speak to them?"

The wounded man nodded.

Penn approached, taking off his hat and fingering it as he looked down at the young man.

"My name is Penn," he said. "I'm sorry to see you hurt so bad, young man."

"I'm dying . . . or so this priest tells me," the bandaged man rasped in a pained voice.

"I think you are," Penn said. "And I'm sorry for you. But what is it you have to tell us?"

"Bethany . . ."

"You know her?"

He nodded again. "Yes. She is in great danger."

"We know that. She was in danger from the moment she was kidnapped."

The young man shook his head, weakly. His red, bleary eyes struggled to stay focused on Penn's face. "No. No danger for her, until now."

"How can you know that?"

"Because it was me . . . who kidnapped her."

Penn and his companions exchanged a startled glance. Sampson said, "Penn, look at his face."

Penn examined the reclining man's features. "My word!" he exclaimed softly. "His face is like Bethany's. Enough that he could be—"

"Her brother," the dying man interjected. "Her half brother, actually. The other child of her father. But not of the same mother. My name is Justin Driver. The last name is my mother's, not my father's."

"You're an illegitimate child?" Penn asked forthrightly.

"Yes. Raised by my mother. Supported by my father as well as he could afford to do, poor as he was. It wasn't much . . . and it wasn't enough. I grew up hungry. Watching my mother suffer from her poverty. Grateful for every scrap, every coin, that my father would give us, but hating him too because it was so little. And he never even acknowledged me. Whenever I saw him, he wouldn't even look at me."

"But for Bethany, it was better," Penn said.

"Yes. She was poor, too, in her early days. But she was sufficiently fed, clothed. Loved. I would ask my mother what the difference was . . . why he cared for her, but not me. She tried to explain what it meant to be illegitimate—'bastard' was the word she used—but it took me a long time to come to really understand it. And it only made me hate him more."

Penn asked, "Did you hate Bethany, too?"

"Yes, in a way. But I was also fascinated by her. Wanted to know her . . . she was my sister, after all. I wanted what she had. Especially after . . ." Driver faded away, his voice just giving out on him. His voice had been growing softer as he went along, and he was visibly weakening. He was indeed dying, and Penn had a strong feeling that this conversation was hastening the process, draining the last of Driver's energy at an accelerated pace. But Driver seemed to want to go on, and in Penn's view, well he should, considering what he'd done.

Penn finished Driver's sentence for him. "You wanted what she had, especially after your father died. When she was sent to live with a wealthy uncle."

Driver nodded almost imperceptibly. He spoke with his eyes closed. "Yes. She had . . . everything. Money. A big home . . . people who cared for her, who would do anything for her. I was jealous, more than I can say. I hated her, but yet still cared for her. I wanted to know my sister . . . wanted her to know about me, who I was. She grew up never knowing I even existed."

"And this led, at last, to a kidnapping scheme."

Another weak nod. "No one was supposed to be hurt. It was a way that I could . . . come into contact with her. Come to know her, and to let her know me . . . and to punish her, too, all at the same time, for having been so much better off than me. And the money . . . there was the money."

"You ought to hang for what you did," Penn said.

"I make no . . . excuse. It was wrong. But no one was supposed to get hurt."

"I'm not sure you know how many have been hurt by what you did."

Tears rose rapidly to the weakening man's eyes. "I hired men . . . to help me. They were told not to let her . . . be hurt. I told them the money would be . . . more than they could hope to ever earn. But they were killed. All of them. Gunned down."

"By other men who came to you with a strongbox, claiming to be the ransom bearers?"

"Yes."

"But the strongbox was empty."

"Yes. And they shot us . . . and took Bethany. They have her now."

"Did one of the men who did this have a large scar on his face?"

Driver's eyes fluttered slowly open.

"Open your eyes! A scar—on the left side," Penn said urgently, tracing his finger in a jagged line down his face. "Like this?"

"Yes," Driver said softly.

"The men who did that were led by two brothers named Dresden. One of them was the trusted foreman of Abel Blain's own ranch. He proved himself a Judas. A betrayer. And a cold-blooded murderer."

Driver closed his eyes again. "It wasn't supposed to happen . . . no one was supposed to die. Bethany was never supposed to be in any real danger."

Sampson pushed up beside Penn and leaned over the slowly dying man. "Open your eyes!" he all but shouted into the pallid face. His voice was so loud that Driver jerked, and groaned terribly from the pain of it.

"Jeff, maybe you shouldn't—"

"No, Penn!" Sampson spat back. "Don't tell me to spare this bastard's feelings! He lies here and grieves because his hired kidnappers were killed. What about the good men who died in Gajardo Canyon? What about my *father*? If not for what this bastard did, my father would be alive!"

Driver groaned again, drawing back from the glaring face looming over him. "Gajardo . . . Canyon . . ."

"He doesn't know what happened there, Jeff," Penn said. "It wasn't him who did it."

"So he doesn't know! I'll tell him, then. There were good men murdered in Gajardo Canyon, you miserable dog! My father among them. Men who were carrying the ransom you demanded, and who died because of it."

Father Mateo came near and touched Sampson's arm. "Please, my son, don't do this!"

Sampson pulled away from Mateo's touch. "Don't tell me what to do, Father! Because of what this man did, my father lies in a shallow grave near Gajardo Canyon. There was no priest to tell him his sins were forgiven, Father. No preacher to pray over his soul."

"Jeff, it was Dresden and his brother who killed your father. Not this man!"

Sampson's fury, though, was stronger than his reason. "That's true enough, Penn, but if not for Bethany being kidnapped, there would have been no ransom, and no reason for the massacre! I hold this man responsible, and I swear to God, I'm going to kill him!"

Sampson lunged and wrapped his hands around Driver's neck.

Chapter Thirty-one

McCutcheon and Penn immediately grabbed Sampson and tried to pull him away. Mateo reached over and peeled Sampson's clutching hands from Driver's throat. Martinez, who had been observing everything from the corner of the room, simply froze in place, unable in his surprise to respond.

Driver, who had been pulled half upright by Sampson, fell back, a horrible sound gurgling from his throat. He grew ashen; his lips quivered and his right cheek twitched.

Samson swore and struggled, then pulled free. But he didn't lunge at Driver again, instead staggering off to the side and slumping to the floor. He began to sob like a child.

McCutcheon said softly to Penn, "It's been too much for him. His father murdered, people trying to shoot us down and rob us . . . even Bethany. He's in love with her, you know."

"I know."

Mateo hovered over Driver, his hands upon him, head bowed, a silent prayer moving his lips.

"I've made many a mistake tonight, Jim," Penn said. "I've been too eager, pushing too hard. We should have locked ourselves up in that hotel room, patched up Jeff's arm as best we could, and gotten some rest. But no. I had to head out and try to push things along."

"None of this is your fault, Penn. You've done a helluva job of keeping us all alive, and the ransom safe."

"It's nonsense, Jim. We owe the ransom's safety more to Martinez than to me."

Oddly, McCutcheon laughed. "Look at us, Jake. You standing there feeling sorry for yourself. Sampson crying like a whipped baby in the corner. Martinez over there so confused he doesn't know what to do. Some hard-as-nails ransom riders, ain't we?"

Penn closed his eyes. "Dear Lord, I'm tired."

"So am I. And the night's far on. I say let's rest while we can. We'll start anew on this thing tomorrow."

Penn thought about it. "We can't, Jim. Remember what Martinez said?" Martinez had mentioned amid his earlier excited talk, that he had seen a figure in the hotel room.

McCutcheon grunted softly. "I'd forgotten for a moment."

"It has to be Dresden, or one of his men. They've tracked us down, and I'll wager you that there's somebody waiting in that room right now, or maybe a letter or note telling us what to do with the ransom."

McCutcheon held silence. "We can't do it, Penn. We can't give that money to Dresden. Not after all he's done."

"We have no choice, Jim."

"He's murdered too many people. For all we know, he's murdered Bethany. It's not right for him to get the money after that."

Penn looked at Sampson, weeping and broken. He watched Mateo, praying over a dying kidnapper who had kindled a bonfire that had flamed up out of his own control. He glanced at Martinez, the good-hearted stranger who had taken on an obligation that was by no estimation anything he had to do.

It all seemed hopeless. Out of control. But he had

to keep a hold on himself, and on the situation, as best he could. For Bethany's sake.

"I'm going to the hotel, Jim."

"Not alone. I'm going with you."

"No reason for that."

"You know there is. Don't argue with me about it."

Penn smiled wearily at his partner. "I won't argue. I'm glad to have you with me tonight, Jim."

"So you're glad I didn't stay put in Black Hill? You're glad I followed you?"

"Sure am."

Father Mateo rose slowly, drawing a blanket across Driver's body, pulling it from his waist until it slowly covered his face.

Sampson rose to follow Penn, McCutcheon, and Martinez out the door, but stumbled. He caught himself, using his wounded arm, and groaned loudly in pain.

"You all right, Jeff?" Penn asked.

"Yeah, yeah, I'm fine." From his voice it was evident he was both hurting and distraught, and fighting to keep on his feet.

"Listen, Jeff, why don't you just stay put," Penn said. "Get some rest. Jim and I can go to the hotel alone."

"I'm coming with you, Penn. I'll not have you two face whoever may be in that room by yourselves."

"There's three of us . . . we'll be fine. Most likely whoever Martinez saw there was either somebody who broke in to steal the money, or it could be a messenger from the Dresden brothers. If so, most likely a note has been left."

"I'm not some child to be left out. I've proven myself as brave and capable as any of you!"

"Of course you have. But there's one difference: You've been shot and we ain't. You need to rest so you can be in shape to help us out when we actually deliver the money."

Sampson snapped again, jabbing a finger at Penn, "You never wanted me here to begin with! You considered me in the way, somebody who just latched on to you without an invitation. Well, then, you just go on without me! I'll go rescue Bethany by myself if I have to!"

"Nobody's going off to rescue Bethany right now, Jeff. We're just going over to the hotel, then coming right back here."

"The hell with you!" Sampson yelled. "Just go off, then! I never should have weighted myself down with you to start with! If I'd just gone on when I first found out about the kidnapping, I might have been there to save my father's life! I might have been able to do something that would have stopped the Dresdens from doing what they did! I might have . . . the hell with it!"

Penn was stern now. "Jeff, you listen to me: Don't you try to do anything on your own. The only way we can safely get Bethany back is to work together and carry that ransom where it's expected. You start being a loose cannon, and you could endanger her even more."

"Always got the answers, don't you, darky! How'd you ever get to be so smart, anyway? You like ordering white folks around . . . is that it?"

This was the first time that Penn had detected any kind of racial hatred in Jeff Sampson. Given the very different attitude that Sampson's father had displayed, Penn was surprised and unable to respond right away.

Mateo stepped toward Sampson. "My son, you are in too great a distress right now. You should cease speaking, calm down, and just rest. You can do your work better when you are rested."

"I'm not your son," Sampson snapped. "I'm not

even a Catholic! I appreciate the bandaging, but I
don't want no sermon."

Mateo said no more. He'd learned through many
hard experiences when it was best simply to remain
silent.

Penn had no more to say, either. He turned away
and, trailed by McCutcheon and Martinez, the latter
of whom was obviously confused by what was going
on, walked out of the door, leaving Mateo and Sampson alone with the body of Bethany Colby's brother.

They walked carefully through the town, which was
as lively as it had been earlier in the evening, and
perhaps more so. Harsh laughter roared in the cantinas, and a few drunken gunshots split the air.

"I didn't know Jeff felt the way he does," McCutcheon said.

"The boy's been through a lot. Lost his father, seen
death and danger all around, and he's worried sick
about Bethany. It's easy to forgive a man a few faults
when he's in such a shape."

"You don't think he'll actually go and try to do
something on his own, do you?"

"No. He's too smart for that. Besides, what could
he hope to do? He can't free her without the ransom."

"Penn, he's got the ransom. It's in the church with
him, remember?"

"I know. But he doesn't know where to deliver it."

"Neither do we."

"Not yet." McCutcheon could almost swear he saw
Penn's eyes twinkle.

The hotel loomed dark and ominously over the
street. They eyed the window of their room but saw
no sign of anyone. They entered the hotel and carefully climbed the stairs. The public areas of the hotel
were empty, and the night man was dozing off in an
office adjacent to the lobby.

They drew their pistols and advanced slowly to the end of the hall. The door to the room was slightly open. Penn nudged it open further with his toe, then peered inside, the barrel of his revolver preceding him.

"Nobody in here," he said. He stepped inside, the others following.

Martinez said something and pointed. Penn didn't understand the words, but the finger aimed him toward something that lay on the end of the bed.

McCutcheon picked it up. It was a scrap of cloth. Penn recognized the fabric at once.

"It's from Bethany's dress," he said.

"There's a folded letter here," McCutcheon said. He picked it up and opened it. "Turn up that lamp, will you?"

Penn cranked up the wick, adding light to the room. McCutcheon moved closer to the lamp and examined the note. "It's a map," he said. "Shows the town, that creek there, those hills to the south. Look there—X marks the spot, as they say."

Penn nodded. "So now we know where to take the money. But does it say when?"

There was writing at the bottom. McCutcheon wondered if it was Keith Dresden's handwriting, or his brother's. The map was quickly scrawled, hard to read. "Dawn," he said. "Delivery at first light. And Jake . . . look there. They want you to do it alone."

Penn looked at the note. "So they do."

"I don't like that, Jake. Why would they want you to deliver the money alone?"

"Dresden's idea, I guess. Me and him didn't much get along. He probably wants to make it as hard on me as he can."

"He may want to kill you. Have you thought of that? You're the only one who was an eyewitness to the massacre in the canyon."

Penn nodded. "I know. But what's to be said about it? If that's the demand, then I have to fulfill it." He looked at his pocketwatch. "In about three hours from now, I guess."

"Yep. But you can forget about going alone, Jake. I won't have it. I'll go with you."

"If you do, then you endanger Bethany's life. Don't worry about me, Jim. I told you before that I believe I've received a promise from above that I'll live to find my sister. In which case, that means I can't get killed carrying this ransom, because I ain't found her yet."

"You may think you've got some prophecy of living. But I ain't so persuaded."

Penn, clearly wanting to talk about this matter no further, took the map and showed it to Martinez, and combining hand motions with what fragments of Spanish he knew, managed to ask him if he could interpret the map. Martinez looked it over and nodded firmly.

"Well, we know where we stand, then," Penn said. "We know when, and we know where. Right now I suggest we go back to the church and get an hour or two of rest. We're all about exhausted."

"How do you reckon they knew to deliver us this map to this room?" McCutcheon asked.

"I suppose somebody must have seen one of us coming out of the hotel. They were probably looking for us while we were looking for them, and we just didn't happen to meet up."

"Well, the torn dress piece confirms that they've really got Bethany, if you know for sure that it's hers," McCutcheon said. "It ain't the same one you've seen before, is it?"

"No. This appears to be torn from the hem. What was brought to us at the old Gajardo Mission was a piece of a sleeve."

"I wonder if they're watching us now," McCutcheon said, glancing at the window, then moving away so he was no longer in the potential line of sight of anyone on the street.

"Could be," Penn said. "But they'll not bother us. Not until they get the money."

"What if they see us go back to the church?" McCutcheon asked. "They might figure out that's where we have the money."

"Then let them figure it out. Let them come get it, if they want. As long as they give us Bethany in return for it."

They left the hotel for the last time, and went to the church as quickly and covertly as they could.

Considering Sampson's volatile emotional state when they left, Penn would not have been overly surprised to find the young man had abandoned them. But, thankfully, he was still there, sound asleep.

"He's sorry for the way he spoke," Mateo told them. "He fretted over it after you were gone. I'm concerned about him. He's undertaken something that is too big and difficult for him."

"He's stronger than he knows," Penn replied. "It takes a challenge to teach us just how strong we can be. But you, Father, look like your own strength is fading tonight. You need rest, like all of us."

"So I do. Do you know now what you need to in order to save the young woman?"

"I do. Tomorrow morning, God willing, we will buy her freedom."

"Then you rest, not me. There will be time for me to sleep later. I'll make sure no one disturbs us, and that the money is safe."

"Thank you, father. Is there a place where I can lie down, then?"

"There are pallets on the floor over there. I laid

them out for you. Your friend Señor Sampson is already making good use of his, you can see."

Penn thanked the priest again and headed for one of the pallets. It was thin and the floor was hard, but he hardly noticed it.

Chapter Thirty-two

She'd cried some at the beginning. Pure terror had caused it, even though she tried to fight it.

But she'd soon given it up, as soon as it became clear to her that her kidnappers intended her no harm. In kidnapping her, the young leader of it had all but admitted to her that they were making a great bluff and hoping that her rich and doting uncle would respond with money. If he refused, they'd not have hurt her. She was sure of it. They'd torn off scraps from her dress when they'd taken her, and put cattle blood on them to frighten Abel Blain, but she'd been able to see that it was all false.

And there'd been something intriguing about the young man behind it all—a sense that she knew him, or should. He'd looked at her oddly, she thought, casting his eyes sidewise at her when he didn't think she would notice. But the looks were not of infatuation, or lust, or any other common motivator that she could think of. There had been something different about that young man, who had so firmly refused to tell her his name or anything about himself, and who had treated her with careful respect throughout.

Bethany Colby had actually come to feel a certain closeness to her original young kidnapper. Part of it, she was sure, had to do with the common tendency of captives to grow to favor their captors. She'd heard enough tales of children taken by Indians, only to turn

Indian themselves, to doubt that such things happened. But there was more to it in this case. She knew that young man somehow. In some vague and indefinable manner, she just knew him.

Bethany paced around the little locked room in which she was a prisoner. She didn't know where she was, exactly; this was a small but sturdy casa belonging to a poor, terrified old farmer who lived alone and who had been frightened nearly to death when they'd taken over his home by force. The general location was somewhere south of the vile town of Castillo. Beyond that, Bethany knew no details.

Except for one. She knew that Keith Dresden, whom Uncle Abel so trusted and relied on, was a devil in human form. He and his brother both. Along with their hired killers, they'd duped and murdered the original band of kidnappers. At first Bethany had thought it was a rescue. The error of that perception had become clear soon enough, though.

Keith Dresden, whom she herself had trusted and even rather liked, had not rescued her but kidnapped her for himself, and for his brother, Cotton. She'd barely known Cotton Dresden—he was a horse trader, she thought, running his horses somewhere over near Black Hill—but Keith she'd known well. Yet he'd betrayed her and her uncle.

Bethany didn't fully understand how it all had come about. She knew bits and pieces: Keith Dresden had started out as the leader of the band of ransom riders her uncle had sent to free her from the clutches of the original kidnappers. There had been a massacre— to her horror, Bethany had heard it attributed to Cotton Dresden—the result being that the Dresden brothers and their hired gunmen took the ransom for themselves.

But something had gone wrong, and the ransom had been carried away, somehow. . . . A black man was involved, someone had mentioned. She'd been unable to ask details; most of what she picked up she'd gained through listening to the conversations of her captors, her ear pressed to the locked door.

And it was that, she'd surmised, that had led the Dresdens to wipe out the original kidnappers and take their place. Only by taking possession of her could the Dresdens hope to have the ransom brought to them.

She stared at the wall and hated Keith and Cotton Dresden. She'd seen their brutality in the massacre of the original kidnappers. She could imagine it must have been worse in the earlier massacre of the ransom riders. She wondered who had died. No doubt her uncle had sent the best men he had on such an important mission. She dreaded learning the identities of the victims, of hearing Jeff Sampson's name.

She heard voices outside, muffled by the heavy barred door that kept her imprisoned. The Dresden brothers, it sounded like . . . arguing. She rose and went to the door, putting her head against it to hear better.

". . . damned sure better work this time!" Cotton Dresden was saying. "You've brought us nigh to the hangman's noose already by the way you've mishandled this whole business!"

Keith Dresden, who Bethany had noted seemed cowed and deferential in the presence of his more domineering brother, was angry and drunk enough to argue back this time.

"Mishandled it? You blame *me*? It was you and the gaggle of fools you hired who failed to kill that darky!"

Bethany surmised from the way Keith Dresden was talking about his brother's men that none of them were present just now. The brothers were there alone. The only other person she knew of that was perpetually in this little house was its owner, the sad and scared little man who was, she thought, locked up in a similar room elsewhere.

"You were right down there with him!" Cotton argued back. "We did the best we could, shooting from above . . . you shouldn't have let him get his hands on the strongbox."

"Hell, Cotton, I done the best I could!"

"Wasn't good enough."

Both brothers sounded drunk, Bethany noted. They had been awake all night. She'd heard their voices, off and on, throughout the long hours of darkness. They'd grown more slurred and argumentative as the night progressed.

"It don't matter now," Keith replied. "That ransom will be carried right to us at first light."

Bethany lifted her brows upon hearing that. So it was at dawn she was to be ransomed! She dropped to her knees and said a prayer that all would go as it should, and that she would remain safe. She prayed as well that the crimes the Dresdens had done would not see them long rewarded. She wanted them dead, and felt no guilt for it.

"You know for sure the letter was delivered? And the piece of the dress was sent?"

"Jimmy told me, and I've done told you: He took it all right into their hotel room and left it on the bed. No way they could miss it."

"But he never saw them get it?"

"No. But how could they miss it?"

"The room was empty when he went in. It may be empty yet. Maybe they moved out of it for some reason! Hell, Keith, the morning may come, and no ransom will show up at all!"

"It'll be here. And my good darky friend Mr. Penn will be bearing it, just as ordered. You wait and see."

Bethany was astonished. It had to be Jake Penn to whom Keith Dresden referred! How did Jake get into the midst of this? He'd not been at the ranch at the time she was kidnapped.

However he'd come into it, she was happy about it. She loved Jake Penn like he was of her own family. He always made her feel safe and happy. She was glad he was bringing the ransom that freed her.

But what she heard next through the door made her feel differently.

"Why'd you insist that the darky bring the money, Keith?" Cotton asked.

"Because it was him who lost it for us in Gajardo Canyon. Because that darky has a smart-talking mouth and uppity ways that rile me to no end. Because he's a darky—that alone. That's reason enough for me. He'll deliver us the money, and we'll give him back pretty little Bethany, just like we promised—but I aim to see Jake Penn go back to Abel Blain strapped to a dragboard."

Bethany's heart seemed to catch in her throat. Jake Penn was going to ride into a massacre of his own.

She felt a wave of fury, her hatred of the Dresden brothers boiling over.

"I don't care what happens to Jake Penn," Cotton said. "All I want is that money."

"You'll have it . . . and I damned sure hope the gunnies you hired will be content with their share of it," Keith answered hotly. "You know there's only two of us and five of them. It won't take a lot of figuring for them to realize they could have the whole pie easy enough, and not just a little slice."

"Don't talk so loud! They're just outside, you fool! They'll hear you and start getting notions."

"I figure they've already come up with the notion. When we get that money, we'll have to pay them off fast, and put distance between us and them. That amount of money is dangerous."

"I can live with half a million dollars' worth of danger."

The argument seemed to have cooled some, probably through the deadening effects of liquor and the lateness of the hour. Bethany herself ached for sleep on one level—for she'd had very little of it since the ordeal began—but there was also a sort of perpetual wild energy that kept her alert and aware, ready to find an escape if one should come. So far none had.

"It's cold in here," Cotton said. "I'm going to go out with the others around the fire."

"Suit yourself."

Bethany heard footsteps, and the opening and closing of a door.

There was now only silence on the other side of the door. Soon, she heard Keith Dresden moving around; it seemed he was muttering to himself. She pressed her ear against the door.

A few moments later she drew back reflexively, with a small gasp.

Keith Dresden stood right on the other side of the door. With her ear pressed to the wood, she'd been only inches away from him.

The bar moved and lifted, and the door opened. Light from the candles burning in the central room of the little casa flickered in and outlined his form. He was looming in the doorway, looking right at her. He had a whiskey bottle in his hand.

He stared at her a few moments, unspeaking, then chuckled. The bottle went up to his mouth. Whiskey sloshed; he swallowed loudly and hissed.

"Ain't going to have you around much longer, Miss Colby," he said, reeking of rotgut. "Supposed to ransom you out of here about first light."

He was telling her nothing she hadn't already learned from eavesdropping, so she said nothing.

"It's a shame, in a way. I'll be glad to have that

ransom, but it'll be sad to see such a beauty gone away from us. I've always thought you were pretty, Bethany. You don't mind me calling you Bethany, do you? It's always laid funny on my tongue, that 'Miss Colby' name.''

She looked away from him, toward the corner. But in the corners of her vision she studied the open door in which he stood, and the room beyond it. Fantasies of flight filled her mind.

The whiskey bottle bobbed up and down again. She wondered why Keith would get himself so drunk so shortly before such an important exchange.

"You know," he said hoarsely. "Cotton told me something yesterday. Made me laugh. He told me he'd always had a little bit of envy for me. He works around horses all day. Hardly ever sees anybody but a bunch of dirty old horse traders and stablemen and such as that. But there I am, right on the ranch, getting to lay eyes on a young filly like you, every time you pass. I'm a lucky man, he told me. And you know, he's right.''

His leer was making her feel slightly nauseated.

He sat the bottle on the floor just inside the door, and swiped the back of his hand across his lips.

He gently eased the door shut behind him. It closed—but Bethany knew the bar was not in place. One push and that door would open.

Keith tottered toward her slowly. She moved away, eyeing him fearfully in the dim light of the candle. "What are you doing?" she demanded. "Don't you come near me!"

"Well! I'd begun to think a cat had got in here!"

She backed away some more. He was getting farther from the doorway the closer he came to her.

He chuckled again. "Don't you want to know what I mean, talking about a cat getting in here?"

"I just want you to leave me alone!"

"You ever heard somebody ask, 'Cat got your tongue?' You ever heard that?" He tittered as his boots lurched forward. She realized how drunk he was.

"Don't you think about touching me!" she exclaimed. At once she regretted it: She'd brought up a possibility that he might seize upon.

He did. "Don't think about touching you? Oh, honey, you don't know what you're asking. I can't help but think about it. You're the prettiest little thing I've seen."

She reached the corner and was trapped.

He advanced, wiping his mouth with his hand again. "I won't be seeing you no more after we turn you over to the ransom boys, you know. I'll not be coming back around your uncle's ranch no more. Can't hardly do that after what I've done, can I?" He cackled again.

"He'll see you dead for what you've done!" Bethany retorted. "You'll not be able to hide from him! He'll hire men to come after you! I know my uncle! He'll do it!"

"I'll be so far away that he'll never be able to track me down. Maybe even out of the country. I intend to enjoy that money. Me and Cotton will pay off them gunmen outside that Cotton hired, and the rest of the money we split down the midst. Nearly a quarter of a million dollars, I'll have! Maybe I can build me a fine house like your uncle's got. Maybe I can live the good life for once, instead of wallowing around in that shack off the bunkhouse."

He was nearly upon her. She smelled his body stench and his whiskey-rotten breath. She'd never thought of Keith Dresden as repellent before—she'd hardly thought of him at all, in fact—but now he seemed the most revolting man she'd ever encountered.

"Come her, girl. Give me a kiss. That's all—just a kiss."

"Never!"

"What can that hurt? It's just a kiss. You don't like me?"

"You're a murderer!"

"I didn't kill nobody. That was Cotton and his boys."

"Who is dead? Were they some of the cowboys from the ranch?"

"Nobody's dead but the ones who kidnapped you. The rest is just Cotton talking big. Come on . . . just one kiss."

"You're a liar!"

"Girl, I'm a lot worse than just that."

He pushed near her. She drew her head back, then rammed it forward, butting her forehead hard against him.

Dresden grunted and staggered back, gripping his nose. She ran at him and shoved him hard, tripping him over. Then she kicked him in the right knee, and finally in the side of the head as he went down. He made strange croaking sounds. Her last kicks pounded him in the forehead, and again in the temple.

She ran out the door and into the central room, heading for the front entrance. She stopped in her tracks, however, when she realized that Cotton Dresden and his hired gunmen were outside.

There was a window at the rear of the room. It was a little small, but just large enough to accommodate her. She opened it and began to scramble out.

Only one thing made her hesitate—on the other side of the room was a barred door, similar to the one that had locked her own room. Inside was the pitiful old man who owned this little farm—her fellow hostage. Though in his case, there was no ransom to be collected.

She should free him . . . shouldn't she? He was old,

and couldn't possibly flee certain death successfully. But they might only punish him. Surely he'd be more likely to survive all this if he did nothing to antagonize his captors . . .

The decision was made for her. Keith Dresden came staggering out of the room, gripping his head, blood dripping from his battered nose. He glared at her and cursed, staggering out in her direction.

She kicked him in the crotch and dropped him. Three more kicks to the head and he moved no more.

Bethany climbed out the window as fast as she could. It was still dark, but dawn would break before long. The time of the ransom exchange . . . if only she could get away before the day came to expose her.

She ran from the house, into the rocks beyond. Pausing, she looked behind her and saw the flicker of light from the campfire burning in front of the house. Men milling around it caused shifts in the beams of light.

She ran farther, deeper into the rocks. When she was thoroughly winded, she stopped again to assess her location. Figuring out the direction in which Castillo lay, she decided to head that way. There was a church there, and a priest. She could find protection, a place to hide.

She set off, running as fast as she could, racing the coming of morning.

Chapter Thirty-three

Keith Dresden rose slowly, pain storming all through him.

He couldn't believe that mere girl had done him such damage! His neck crackled, his knees too, and his groin throbbed so that he could hardly stand. That kick had not only been injuring, but humiliating.

She was gone now. He pondered that, letting the significance sink in. No hostage . . . no reason to pay ransom.

He swore softly, realizing how great a mistake he'd made in letting her get past him. He saw the open window and knew how she'd gotten out. She was probably running out there somewhere in the dark, in which direction he couldn't begin to suppose.

Castillo, probably. That's where he'd head.

He knew what he ought to do: Go out there and tell Cotton and the others what had happened. They could fan out, track her down, and find her in time to make the exchange for ransom when the sun came up.

But the embarrassment of it! How could he admit to them—to Cotton in particular—that he'd been bested by a shrimp of a girl?

No, he'd track her down alone. He could save at least a little face that way.

Though it hurt quite a lot to do it, and though the fit was so tight he could hardly make it through without taking off his hide, he managed to wiggle out the window. With no way to track her in the dark, he played his hunch and headed in the direction of Castillo. With luck he'd detect her before dawn. If not, he'd surely be able to track her after first light . . . wouldn't he?

He wondered what would happen if she got away. All that ransom, gone. All that they'd done, and no payday.

Cotton would kill him.

He hurried on, determined to find her.

An hour later, the sky began to lighten. The sun edged up over the western hills and poured a slanting light across the Mexican landscape.

Across a barren expanse a lone rider advanced, leading a packhorse on which a strongbox was strapped. He looked around hesitantly, wondering if he was being watched.

Jake Penn halted his horse and paused to take a few deep breaths. This was more nerve-wracking than he'd anticipated. He almost wished he'd not succeeded in persuading McCutcheon and the others to stay behind. It was mighty lonely out here.

He was concerned about the Dresdens and their gunmen. They might carry the deal through as their own demands directed, or everything might take a deadly turn.

Penn didn't care about turning over such a large amount of money. It wasn't his, anyway. His only concern was for Bethany.

Even more than the Dresdens, he worried about the other desperados who might make one last try for the money. Enough had tried to get the money already.

What a tragic irony it would be to come this close to ransoming Bethany, only to have the money spirited away by outsiders.

Penn turned his head suddenly. He thought he'd

heard something up in the rocky hills to his right. Maybe somebody was watching him. Someone who had followed from Castillo, or stationed themselves here for ambush.

Or maybe it was no one at all. He was edgy, over-reacting to every noise.

He hoped this would all be over soon.

He rode on, hoping that he was following the map accurately.

But as he advanced, something began to nag at him. What if, somehow, there was falseness at the root of all this? What if they really didn't have Bethany? What if—as bad as it was to think it—she had been killed in the raid against the original kidnappers? She might have died without the ill-fated Driver being aware of it.

That scrap of cloth in the hotel room didn't neces-sarily mean Bethany was still living.

Penn eyed the hills, thinking hard. Maybe one slight divergence from the original plan might be worth-while. It was chancy, in a way . . .

He remained where he was, unsure what to do as the sun climbed and time slipped away.

Cotton Dresden was a man who grew angry easily and often, but his rage at this moment was greater than any he had felt in years, perhaps ever at all.

He was inside the room in which the old farmer was held, stalking back and forth before the terrified man. With Cotton was one of his hired gang, a mixed breed of white, Indian, and Mexican blood. He spoke Spanish, and translated Cotton's blistering interroga-tion of the old man.

"He's bound to have heard something!" Cotton de-clared. "The girl got out somehow—Keith wouldn't have done it on purpose. He opened that door for

some reason, and she got away. He'd have raised a
fuss, done something!"

The translator questioned the old man sharply. The
fellow, near tears, replied in a wavering voice, his
hands uplifted pleadingly.

"He says he heard something, but he wasn't sure
what it was," the translator said to Cotton. "Maybe a
fight of some kind."

"So we're to believe that this little scrap of a girl
was able to outfight Keith. I don't buy that."

"Maybe it wasn't a fight he heard," the other said.

"What do you mean?"

"Maybe Keith let her out so he could have a good
time with her."

Cotton thought that over. With all his wicked nature, one fault he lacked: He'd never been a lustful
man. The possibility that Keith might have attempted
a liaison with the little girl simply hadn't crossed his
mind.

"It would explain why they went out the window,"
he said. "He wouldn't have wanted us outside to see
that he'd let her go."

"Well . . . where is she now?"

"Maybe he's still got her out there somewhere."

"Hell with that! It's time to go fetch the ransom!
How we going to do it without a hostage!"

The other shrugged. But if he seemed nonchalant,
it was a mask: Without the collection of that ransom,
no one, not the Dresdens or their hired guns, would
make so much as a peso.

"What happens now?" the translator asked Cotton.

He received no answer. Cotton Dresden was staring
at the trembling old man, deep in thought.

Jake Penn hid behind a stand of rocks on a hillside
ledge, looking down on the little farm below. He felt
a certain relief because the surrounding area matched

the map, thus verifying that he'd come to the right location. But he was also concerned. Some inner warning was sounding.

He wondered why he'd been instructed to come here alone. Given the danger that others might intercept and steal the ransom money on the way to this place, wouldn't the kidnappers have preferred that the money be well guarded? And why did they care whether he or one of the others brought in the money?

For some reason, they wanted to isolate Jake Penn in particular. Jake could think of only one explanation: They wished to eliminate the sole survivor of the Gajardo Canyon massacre, the only man who could give first-hand testimony about what had happened there.

Penn was glad he hadn't ridden directly into the valley below. There was a dangerous undercurrent here that demanded he give himself whatever edge he could.

The only edge was control of the ransom money. If he could contrive a situation that would tie the ransom money to his own survival, he might have a chance to live . . . at least for a little longer.

He looked up. "Lord," he prayed, "I asked You long ago to let me live long enough to find my sister. I felt You answered me that You would. I sure hope, Lord, that I didn't hear You wrong about that."

Penn began glancing around the hillside. Maybe he could hide the strongbox somewhere they wouldn't be likely to find unless he revealed where. They'd have to keep him alive then. If they were going to hold Bethany hostage, then maybe he could hold the ransom itself hostage in turn.

Taking care to keep low and out of view of anyone who might appear on the flats below, Penn explored the hillside, poking about through the rocks.

He stopped, peered closer, and slowly began to smile. *Ah, yes. This will do.*

He headed back to get the strongbox, then ducked suddenly—men had emerged from the little casa down on the flats. Though he was quite far away, he could see that one of them was Cotton Dresden. He could see no sign of Keith, nor of Bethany. Maybe Keith was inside, standing guard over her.

He had to move fast. The time for meeting the enemy was at hand. He only hoped he could find a way to pull this off and come out with Bethany and himself still alive on the other end of it.

"Where is that darky?" Cotton Dresden said aloud. It had been ten minutes or more since Penn had spotted him emerging from the house below. "The sun's rising high, and he still ain't come."

"Maybe he decided to take that money for himself," one of the hired gunmen suggested.

"Hell, he ain't going to do that. Not after all he's gone through to get it here. Keith says that the darky is close to the girl and would probably do anything to save her."

"But now we ain't got the girl to give him. He won't turn over that ransom without her."

"He won't have any choice. There's a lot more of us than there is of him. Once he shows himself, that money is ours."

"What will you do with him, once it's done?"

"Kill him. Keith was set on it because he don't like him. Me, I figure it can't hurt to have him dead, considering what he saw us do at Gajardo Canyon."

"I'd like to be the one to shoot him, if that's all right with you."

"Suit yourself. Keith ain't here to claim the right for himself, so it's your honor if you want it."

"Look—there he comes."

Sure enough, a lone rider had appeared at the low point of the hill's crest, a natural gap through which ran the horse trail that was the only access into the little valley. Cotton Dresden cupped his hands over his eyes and studied the newcomer.

"It's the darky, sure enough," he said.

"Alone?"

"Appears to be. He's leading a packhorse, too . . . wait a minute. Wait a minute! There's no box on that packhorse. No bags, nothing!"

"He ain't got the ransom?"

"Not unless he's got it stuffed in his saddlebags. Damnation! I'll kill him myself!"

"Best wait until we hear him out," the other suggested. "Maybe he's got the money hid somewhere."

Chapter Thirty-four

Jake Penn hoped he looked calmer than he felt. His heart was about to hammer out of his chest. He rode slowly, looking as nonchalantly as possible at the gaggle of rough men awaiting him ahead. There was still no sign of Keith Dresden, or Bethany. They'd probably hold her inside until the last moment.

As instructed in the note accompanying the map that had led him here, Penn had left all his weapons behind. He rode with no protection at all, and was aware that the emptiness of the packsaddle on the horse he led was already duly noted by the Dresden gang.

He caught himself hoping that Sampson and McCutcheon had disobeyed his strict orders and had followed him. He'd certainly like it if they were somewhere up on the rocks, covering him.

Cotton Dresden walked toward him. He wore a Colt pistol and had a sawed-off shotgun in his left hand, dangling carelessly. Penn knew, though, that he could whip up that shotgun in less than a blink and cut him in half if he wanted.

Penn and Cotton stared at one another a few moments.

"Where's your brother?" Penn asked.

"Ain't here just now."

"So I can see." Penn looked around. "Where's Bethany Colby?"

"Who gave you leave to come asking questions, African? I've got a question for you: Where's the money?"

"Hid."

The shotgun flashed up. "What do you mean, hid?"

"Exactly what I said. It's hid. And not a living soul in this world knows where it is except me. And I ain't telling it until I see Miss Bethany safe and sound."

"I'll blow you out of that saddle, boy."

"Go ahead. I'll be dead, but you'll be broke. You'll not find that money if you kill me."

There was more bluff than truth in what Penn said. In fact the money wasn't far away, and with effort, Dresden and the gang would eventually find it. But it was crucial not to let that fact be known.

"You can't go changing the arrangements on us, boy. We'll not be pushed around by some uppity darky."

"All I can tell you is that you better respect this uppity darky if you want to get that money," Penn said. "Show me Bethany. Now."

"Get down off that saddle."

"No."

"You're defying me?"

"That's the size of it. Show me Bethany, or I walk."

Cotton stood there, glaring at the impudent horseman. Penn wondered if he'd pushed too hard, too far. Cotton's jaw twitched, then he turned and stomped back toward the cabin and stormed inside.

The hired gunmen looked at one another—odd glances, Penn thought, as if they were uncertain about something—and then back at him. And at the burdenless packhorse.

The cabin door opened again and Cotton emerged. He was pushing before him a weeping old Mexican man who seemed almost too scared to stand. Cotton pointed his hogleg at the man's ear.

"Who is this?" Penn asked.

"A man who'll be dead unless you go fetch that ransom right now."

"Wait a minute," Penn said. "Wait a minute. I came here to ransom Bethany Colby. Where is she?"

"You forget about the girl," Cotton shot back. "It's this man's life you'd best be concerned about now."

Penn shook his head. He was growing unnerved despite all his mighty efforts to not show it. "This was not the bargain. That money wasn't sent to save anyone but Bethany Colby."

"Are you willing to see this old man die, nigra? Think about that!"

"Let him go . . . he has no part of this."

"The money, or he dies."

"I can't give it to you! It wasn't sent for him!"

"Then watch him die." Cotton pulled back both hammers of the sawed-off.

"Wait!" Penn said. "Wait . . . don't kill him."

"You'll cooperate, then?"

Jake Penn seldom encountered traps that he couldn't work his way out of, but this time he was stymied. Cotton Dresden had twisted this situation into a configuration Penn had not expected.

He had no idea where Bethany was; the implication of all this was that she was probably not here at all. Maybe she'd died in the same massacre that had wiped out her original kidnappers. Maybe she'd escaped on her own.

The grating thing was, none of it mattered just now. Penn couldn't let that old man die.

"All right," he said, raising his hands in surrender. "All right . . . I'll go get the money."

"Go get it . . . no, you'll take me to it. I'll not let you go sneaking out of sight now."

Cotton turned to his hired band. "Come on . . .

follow us. Keep your guns ready. This boy's about to lead us to our money at last."

On the far side of the hills, Jim McCutcheon rode beside a very sore and worn-out Jeff Sampson. Martinez rode slightly to their rear.

"I hope we're doing the right thing," McCutcheon said. "Penn was right firm about us not following."

"We have to follow," Sampson replied. "Just like at the start of it all. We had to follow the ransom riders then, and we've got to follow Penn now."

McCutcheon glanced back at Martinez. "I'm not sure our friend has as much spirit to do this as he did at the beginning, when he was shooting snipers in the woods just to do us a favor."

"This isn't really his fight . . . I don't know why he's done all he has. I'd say it was for the money, except that he had plenty of opportunity to take it in Castillo, and he didn't."

"There's evil men in the world," McCutcheon said. "Maybe there's good ones, too."

"I sure hope so. Are we sure we're going the right way?"

"I got a good look at the map. This is the way. See them hills ahead? Just beyond them, I believe, is where the ransom is to be delivered.

"I wonder if Penn's done it already?"

"Maybe. Let's get into the hills and see. Whatever we do, let's not let the Dresdens and their gang see us."

Cotton Dresden had turned custody of the old man over to his hirelings. He walked closely behind Penn, the shotgun now trained on Penn's back.

They were climbing into the rocks, Penn doing so with ease and long strides. Cotton was having a harder time of it, puffing and straining.

"Hold up!" he said at length. "Where you taking us?"

"To the money," Penn replied. He was not bluffing this time. He'd hidden the money deep in a cavern he'd stumbled across while looking for a good stashing place. He'd take no chances with an innocent old man's life. He intended to place the money right into Cotton Dresden's hands. He hoped Abel Blain would be a big enough man to understand why he had to do it.

"What kind of place did you hide it in?"

"A cave. You can get into it from up there, on that ledge."

They'd abandoned the horses below because of the steepness of the slope. The hired guns were falling behind because the old man simply couldn't keep up. They were half carrying the fellow as it was.

"Got to rest a minute," Cotton panted.

"Tell me . . . where is Bethany Colby?" Penn asked.

"Forget her."

"Why not tell me? You're going to get your money anyway. I've risked my neck for her. A lot of men died trying to save her. Why not just tell me?"

Cotton shrugged. "All right. I don't know where she is. She got away from us."

"And Keith went after her?"

"I think so. I don't know where he is, either."

Penn hoped Bethany was all right.

"You rested enough now?" he asked.

Cotton Dresden didn't look at all rested, but with some reluctance, he nodded.

They pressed on.

The cave entrance was small and had a downward slope, sort of a throat into the hillside.

"What did you do?" Dresden asked. "Drop the money in there?"

"I didn't drop it," Penn said. "I crawled in. There's

wood in there, by the way, and coal oil torches. This cave has already been used by somebody for storage."

"Do tell. Well . . . let's get in there. I sure as hell wish you'd found an easier place to hide the money."

"I made do with what I could find."

"If this is a trick, boy, I'll blow you in half. Even if that does mean I never find the money."

Penn didn't believe that, but he'd take no chances. Besides, he had no tricks in mind.

Penn went in first. Cotton followed, doing a more nimble job of it than Penn had expected.

The cavern, small at its entrance, was much larger just inside. Both Penn and Cotton could stand without having to stoop at all.

"There's the torches I mentioned," Penn said, nudging with his toe at a pile of long-handled torches made with tin bottles with wicks mounted on the end of poles. There was a jug of coal oil sitting nearby.

"Fire a couple of those up," Cotton ordered.

Penn did the job, pouring the bottles of coal oil and lighting the wicks. The light wasn't bright, but it was sufficient to reveal dark marks on the cavern ceiling, showing where this cave had been much used and explored over the years. The flickering light revealed various casks and barrels stacked back into the cave. Penn wasn't sure who would have stored goods in this cave, or why. Maybe smugglers, perhaps freighters using the cave as a temporary kind of warehouse.

"How far back?" Cotton asked.

"Not very far. Fifty, sixty feet."

"This better not be a trick."

"No trick. You've got my word."

With the torches uplifted, they advanced into the cave. It was irregularly sized, and although they would not have to penetrate the cave far, the sense of claustrophobia pounded them both.

"Where is it?" Cotton growled impatiently.

"Over there," Penn said. He pointed and held out his torch.

Its light played over the strongbox, sitting at the brink of a steep downdrop in the cavern.

"Oh, yes. There's a sweet sight!" Cotton said softly. "Half a million dollars!"

He ordered Penn to stand against the cavern wall while he advanced to the strongbox. He knelt and stroked it, smiling over it with a glitter in his eye.

"You got a key?" he asked.

"No," Penn said. "I figured Keith had it. He led the group of us at the start."

Cotton shoved the strongbox toward Penn. "Break the lock open," he said. "I want to see that money."

"I'll need a tool," Penn said.

Cotton waved his torch around until he found a scrap of metal on the cave floor, apparently part of an old hinge.

"Pop it with that," he said.

Penn went to work. It was difficult, as the metal scrap was not at all an effective prybar, but if this was what Cotton wanted, so be it.

Penn was sweating and exhausted by the time the lock gave way. He glanced up at Cotton.

"Back away," Cotton ordered, a greedy glare in his eyes.

Penn did. Cotton used the short muzzle of the sawed-off to flip back the lid.

The torchlight spilled over the cash filling the box in neatly bound stacks.

"Hallelujah!" Cotton Dresden whispered. "Glory be!"

"There's your money," Penn said. "Now let the old man go. And me, too."

Cotton didn't even hear him. He was pulling out the stacks of money, almost in tears.

Penn spoke more loudly. "Let me and the old man go," he said. "You've got what you wanted."

Cotton put the money back into the box and glared at Penn. "Let you go?" he said. "No. No. You were at Gajardo Canyon. You should have died there, but you didn't. We'll make up for that little wrong turn right now."

He raised the shotgun.

There was not even a split second available for Penn to think through what was happening. He knew that he'd be shot as quickly as Cotton Dresden could pull the trigger. So he didn't give him time. Penn lunged forward, wrenched the shotgun away, and shoved Cotton back, hard.

Cotton, howling in surprise and fright, fell over the edge of the steep slope just behind the strongbox. He tumbled down into the darkness, setting off a small rockslide after him. Some of the ground beneath the strongbox gave way, and the box tumbled down after Cotton, spilling stacks of bills all the way.

Penn picked up a dropped torch and ran over to the edge. Looking down, he held the torch out.

He could barely make out Cotton's form lying far down the slope. Thirty feet down, Penn estimated.

"Are you alive?" he called out.

"My leg .. ." Cotton said. "I think it's broke."

Good, Penn thought. He hoped it hurt. Aloud, he said, "Can you climb up again?"

"No . . . go get help! Get the others . . ."

"All right," Penn said. "I'll go now." He threw the torch down. "So you won't be in the dark," he explained.

The flame set one of the bundles of money on fire about halfway down the slope. Penn watched it burn and laughed to himself.

He headed toward the entrance of the cave.

*   *   *

McCutcheon and Sampson lay on their bellies, watching the cluster of men gathered on a ledge farther down on the same ridge of hills.

"Do you see Penn?" McCutcheon asked.

"No," Sampson said. "Why are they gathered there?"

"I don't know. Wait . . . that might be a cave entrance. Or maybe it's just a shadow. I can't tell."

"Bethany's not there, either. Or either of the Dresden brothers."

"Who's the old man?"

"I don't know. But he doesn't look glad to be there. Look at him . . . he keeps falling. There . . . they just let him slump to the ground."

"I don't understand this," McCutcheon said.

"Jim . . ."

McCutcheon didn't answer, distracted by the scene below.

"Jim, Martinez is gone."

McCutcheon looked back over his shoulder. Martinez had been behind them when they crawled to this hidden overlook. But now he was nowhere to be seen.

"Why would he leave?" Sampson asked.

"I guess he's had enough," McCutcheon replied. He couldn't worry about Martinez right now. He turned his attention back to the gathering of men on the ledge, and wondered where Penn was just now.

When Jake Penn emerged from the cave alone, the hired gunmen weren't sure what to make of it.

"Where's Dresden?" demanded one, training a pistol on Penn. Penn might have come out armed himself, had he chosen, but he'd opted to leave the shotgun hidden inside the cave. There were simply too many gunmen outside to make it wise to take them on with only two barrels' worth of shot.

"He's gone," Penn said. "He took the money and headed out through a different opening."

"The hell!"

"I'm telling you the truth," Penn said as convincingly as he could. "He's cheated you."

"You're a liar," one of the men said. "You've killed him in there."

"I'm telling you, he's gone," Penn said. Just then he noted the old man lying unmoving among the rocks. "Is he . . ."

"Never mind about him," the man said. "You tell us what happened to Dresden. Where's the money?"

"He's taken it, I tell you," Penn insisted. "If you want your cut, you'd best head across this ridge. He's found a way out the other side."

"You're a liar, and we've got no more use for you," one of the others said. He pulled a pistol, aimed it at Penn's head, and pulled the trigger.

"Do you see that!" McCutcheon declared as he saw the man aim at Penn's head. "Dear Lord . . ." McCutcheon leveled his rifle as Sampson did the same. They opened fire just before the man's pistol cracked below, the outlaw startled by the shots. Two of the gunmen fell around him.

McCutcheon saw, meanwhile, that Penn was not down. The shot had missed him at best, grazed him at worst. He'd ducked into the cave.

The other gunmen scattered. One tried to hide among the rocks, but Sampson brought him down. Two others ducked into the cavern after Penn. McCutcheon swore softly; this was an unintended event. The idea had been to drive the gunmen away from Penn, not send them in after him.

It was evident that the old man was not a concern. He lay completely unmoving. Even from a distance, McCutcheon was sure the man was dead.

McCutcheon aimed and fired at one last gunman who was shooting wildly back in their direction, his shots glancing high. McCutcheon did better. The man fell.

There were now no gunmen in the valley. Penn was in the cave, two outlaws having run in after him.

McCutcheon and Sampson rose and began snaking their way through the rocks toward the place where Penn had disappeared, hoping they would not be too late to save him.

Penn honestly didn't know what he would do. He'd hoped that he could bluff the gunmen and send them scrambling over the ridge in a goose chase after Cotton Dresden. He'd not anticipated being shot at, and certainly not being pursued back into the cave.

He wondered if they were after him, or just after the money. He also wondered if he thought he'd heard shots fired from father down the ridge.

McCutcheon, Sampson, and Martinez maybe?

Penn had no time to ponder this. He raced back through the cave, snatching up the still-burning torch he had dropped on the way out. He heard the two gunmen behind him, stumbling through, tripping over some of the casks and crates in the cavern.

Penn cast down the torch, realizing it exposed him. But ahead he saw a faint flicker—torchlight rising from the slope down which Cotton had fallen. Penn remembered the torch he'd tossed down after him in a moment of frankly unjustified mercy toward a man who'd just tried to kill him.

Penn could think of only one way to escape being overrun by the two pursuing gunmen. Without allowing himself to think, he sprinted for that steep slope and let himself slide down it, toward the torch. He managed to hook it with his hand as he went by, but he began to tumble farther down the rocks, and lost it on the way. The coal oil flame remained lit, though.

Penn hit the bottom of the slope at about the same place that Cotton had. The breath was knocked out of him, but he didn't seem to have suffered much damage.

The torch lay nearby. He picked it up and looked around . . .

Cotton was gone. Penn was astonished. The man had said his leg was broken!

Penn turned, wondering what he should do now, where he should go. The torch was a danger to him, but the idea of snuffing it seemed intolerable.

Penn saw the battered strongbox lying not far away, bundled money spilled out all around it.

Maybe Cotton actually *had* found another way out. Maybe Penn could find it, too . . .

He turned, and sensed more than actually saw the open space before him. A great pit, almost impossible to see in the dim flicker of the torch. Penn's boot-toes actually probed out over the edge; he teetered, almost falling, dropping the torch by accident.

He saw it fall, watched light play over the sides of the well-like pit . . . and saw, in a brief, passing flash, the form of Cotton Dresden, hanging onto a rocky outcrop twenty feet down. His pale face, grimacing in horror, was revealed by the light of the torch as it fell by him.

Penn managed to launch himself backward, away from the pit rather than into it. There he lay, breathless from the shock of nearly falling, and horrified by the sight of poor Dresden hanging there hopelessly, out of reach of help . . .

He heard Dresden's feeble cry as he finally lost his grip and fell.

Penn closed his eyes and shuddered, imagining how it must have been . . . Dresden dragging himself along on his broken leg, looking for escape, rolling over the side of the unseen pit, catching himself by chance on that outcrop . . . and then having nothing more to do than wait for his strength to fail him.

Penn did not move. For the moment, he'd simply lost the will.

He heard noise, a tumbling sound, a grunting voice . . .

One of the two pursuing gunmen had fallen down the steep slope.

Penn held his breath, waiting for the man to rise. He did, and called to the second gunman, asking for help.

Penn wondered if the man had any idea that the much-sought ransom money was scattered all about his feet.

The sudden echo of gunshots above made Penn jump, startled. The gunman who had fallen down the slope stood no more than fifteen feet away from him, swearing in surprise. He took a few steps back reflexively.

Penn heard his scream, echoing, as the hidden pit claimed one more victim.

From above, Penn heard a familiar voice, calling his name and speaking Spanish.

"Martinez!" Penn called back. "Martinez . . . I'm down here!"

As the morning sun climbed the sky above them, Penn, McCutcheon, and Sampson sat on the ledge outside the cave's entrance. A rope found at the casa below had served Penn's rescue. He said a prayer of thanks for the gift of open space, of light, of fresh air.

He was glad to be out of the cave, and glad to be alive.

They watched as Martinez sat near the still body of the old man who had died while held hostage . . . died, as best could be told, of nothing more than the relentless fright of being a prisoner.

Sampson had talked to Martinez a few minutes before.

"It must have been a shock for him to look down here and see his own elderly uncle as a prisoner of that gaggle of devils," Sampson said. "That's why he vanished on us, Jim. When he saw it was his own uncle being made such a victim, he had bigger fish to fry than we did, and took off to do something about it."

"Well, he was too late to save his uncle, but he did manage to save me," Penn said. "If he hadn't come into the cave and gunned down that last man, the chances are good that I would have been found." He paused, then pointed at the damaged but still mostly intact strongbox they had rescued from the cave right along with himself. "And we wouldn't still have Abel's money—or most of it, anyway—to carry back to him."

"But no Bethany," Sampson said. "She's dead, I fear."

"I don't think so," Penn replied. "Cotton told me she'd simply vanished, and Keith Dresden along with her. I'm hoping she made an escape and Keith pursued her . . . and that she won the chase."

"In any case, we've not succeeded in rescuing Bethany Colby," McCutcheon said. "We simply don't know where she is, or if she is . . . well, if she's even alive."

"So what's next?" Sampson asked.

Penn drew in a slow breath. "I suppose what's next is to go back to Abel, and give him his money. Then maybe we can begin to try to track down what has become of Bethany."

"Maybe we should look for her before we carry the money back," Sampson said.

"An excellent notion!"

A voice from above made all of them start and look up.

At the top of a bluff above them, Keith Dresden

stood with Bethany Colby trapped in his grasp, a
wicked knife to her throat. She stared down at the
men below her with horror in her eyes, but also with
anger and defiance.

Penn stood. "Let her go, Dresden!"

"Oh, no. No. Not until that strongbox down there
is mine!" he said. "I don't know what's happened
here . . . I don't know where my brother or the others
are . . . but I want that money. I've got my hostage,
and if you want her back alive, you'll send that money
up to me right now."

To the surprise of all, it was Bethany who spoke
next. Ignoring the press of the blade point to her
throat, she said, "I've got a better idea, Mr. Dresden.
Rather than bringing the money up to you, why don't
you go down to it?"

She gave a sudden turn and wrenched away from
his grip. Keith Dresden, utterly surprised by the move,
lost his balance and his grip, and fell from atop the
bluff straight toward Penn.

Penn's instinct was to try to catch the man. But he
managed to ignore the impulse.

Keith Dresden hit the ledge hard, and was knocked
out cold.

Bethany Colby stood above, her dress tattered and
filthy, her hair a shapeless mass around her head . . .
and as Penn looked up at her, she raised her fist
slowly, briefly. It was a gesture of triumph.

After all the money, the effort, the death and danger, Bethany Colby had ended up rescuing herself.

Chapter Thirty-five

Jake Penn couldn't hold back a tear, even though it embarrassed him. He was standing in the front room of Abel Blain's mansion, McCutcheon at his side. Penn always had tended to get choked up when he saw other people crying.

Abel Blain was bawling openly, shamelessly, as he clutched his niece to him and let out the emotions that he'd bottled up inside of him for days. From time to time he would pull back from her a little, without releasing her, and look at her just to verify again to himself that she really was alive, and really was home.

More astonishing than that, most of the ransom money was at home, too. All that was gone was that which had been lost when the strongbox tumbled down the slope inside the cave. That, plus another twenty thousand dollars that Abel had insisted should be divided evenly between Jake Penn, Jim McCutcheon, Jeff Sampson, and Luis Martinez.

Martinez was out on the ranch grounds somewhere, walking about in the sheer excitement of sudden wealth.

Another five thousand would soon be sent to Father Mateo in the church in Castillo, for use of the church. Abel Blain was a grateful man.

"He's happy to have his gal back," McCutcheon said. "So why all the weeping? Makes me uncomfortable."

"I suppose he wasn't sure he'd ever see her again."

"Know what I keep thinking about, Jake?"

"I can guess. The money."

"That's right. Ten thousand between us. We're well off now. We could live the good life. We could go into business, or ranching or something."

Penn shook his head. "No. That money is going to help me continue to look for my sister. It gives me a new hope that I'll actually be able to succeed."

"Well, we have to do something special with it. Surely we won't just keep on drifting and sleeping on the ground like before."

"Let's talk about that another time, Jim. Right now I'm content just to enjoy seeing Abel and Bethany back together."

"This one almost killed us, Jake."

"You couldn't come much closer, could you?"

"There's going to be a lot of grieving here, you know, after the happiness of the reunion settles down."

"Yes . . . and a lot of bitter cowboys. They'll not forgive Keith Dresden for what he helped bring about in Gajardo Canyon."

"Where is he now?"

"Locked up in some shed in the back."

"Ah, yes. I know the place," McCutcheon said.

"They'll haul him elsewhere, of course, to some real jail in a larger town. And then, God have mercy on his soul."

"They'll convict him, huh?"

"If it ever gets that far."

"What do you mean?"

"Abel plans to let his cowboys be the ones to transport Dresden into custody."

McCutcheon thought about that. "Oh," he said.

Jeff Sampson was as sick and weak as a man could be. His wounded arm had festered, a fever had overtaken him, and he was so exhausted that he could hardly move a hand. It was as if he'd kept himself from a physical breakdown by the sheer force of will.

He was asleep when Penn and McCutcheon climbed the stairs to tell him goodbye. With ten thousand dollars between them there was no longer a dire need to find work. They were free to move on, and would.

"Should we wake him?" Penn asked.

"No," McCutcheon said. "Let's let him get his rest. You know, I think all this was maybe harder on him than on anybody."

"Lost his father, almost lost the lady he loves."

"Think she might love him, too?"

"You never know. I tell you, though: She owes him quite a debt of thanks. He went through a lot of hell just because he wanted to see her rescued."

Penn reached down and patted the sleeping Sampson on the shoulder. "Goodbye for now, my friend. We'll come back around to see you one of these days. Good luck with Bethany."

"Ready to go, Penn?"

"I'd like to say farewell to Martinez first. Let's go out and find him. Then I guess we need to say goodbye to Abel and Bethany, too."

"I'm ready to get away from Texas, I think."

"Me, too. It's just too dang close to Mexico, and I've had all of Mexico I care to have for a long, long time."

"Where do you want to go?"

"Well, there were those clues we picked up that Nora might have been in Kansas or thereabouts. Maybe we should go check them out."

"On the move again. It never stops for us, does it?"

"Never does."

A day after Penn and McCutcheon rode away from the Blain ranch, a delegation of Blain's cowboys shoved a very edgy, scared, and tied-up Keith Dresden onto a horse and rode him off, under heavy guard, toward Black Hill. The plan, ostensibly, was to turn him over into the town marshal's custody. The marshal would in turn pass Dresden on to higher authorities to face a long string of official charges stemming from his many crimes in connection with the Bethany Colby kidnapping.

The riders came back to the ranch much sooner than might have been expected, though. They told a sad tale. It seemed that another band of riders, even more heavily armed and wearing masks, had intercepted them and taken the prisoner. Despite all their best efforts, they told Abel Blain, those sorry intruders had taken poor old Keith Dresden and strung him up to a cottonwood limb. The unfortunate fellow died hard, they said.

"It's mighty sad," the man reporting the news said to Abel Blain.

"Isn't it, though," Blain said. "Truly a tragedy. They buried him, I guess?"

"You know, I think they just left him hanging."

"Oh, well," Blain replied. "I suppose the decent thing would be to cut him down. Dignity and all that."

"Whatever you say, boss."

"Thank you . . . but on the other hand, I reckon there's no hurry. I mean, why deprive the crows and buzzards of a good opportunity? They got to eat just like the rest of us."